Lethe Press
Amherst, MA

Acres of Perhaps

Stories and Episodes

Will Ludwigsen

Published in 2018 by Lethe Press, Inc.
6 University Drive | Suite 206 | PMB #223
Amherst, MA 01002
www.lethepressbooks.com | lethepress@aol.com
ISBN: 978-159021-365-0

Credits for original publication appear in the Story Notes.

Set in Neutraface and Goudy Old Style.
Interior design: Will Ludwigsen
Cover design: Will Ludwigsen
Cover image: David Lally

LIBRARY OF CONGRESS
CATALOGING-IN-PUBLICATION DATA
FORTHCOMING

For my mother, Dianne Hall, who always told strangers three things: we're geniuses, we're from New York, and her son is an author. I'm not sure about the first, but she's the reason I'm the second and third. She taught me by example how to live in the world of dreams even when terrible people keep trying to pull you out.

Contents

Acres of Perhaps

If you were a certain kind of person with a certain kind of schedule in the early 60s, you probably saw a show that some friends of mine and I worked on called Acres of Perhaps. By "certain kind of person," I mean insomniac or alcoholic; by "certain kind of schedule," I mean awake at 11:30 at night with only your flickering gray-eyed television for company.

With any luck, it left you feeling that however weird your life was, it could always be weirder. Or at least more ironic. We would have settled for that in those earnest days.

They have conventions about our show where I bloviate on stage about what the aliens represented or how hard it was to work with Claude Akins or what we used to build the Martian spaceships. Graduate students write papers with titles like "Riding the Late Night Fantastic: Acres of Perhaps and the Post-War American Para-Consciousness." I'm now an ambassador for the show and for my friends, and I'm the worst possible choice.

I wasn't the one with the drive to create big things like our producer Hugh Kline, and I damned well wasn't the one with the vision and the awe like David Findley. I was just Barry Weyrich, the guy who wrote about spacemen in glass bubble helmets, who put commas in everyone's scripts, who never had writer's block, who grimaced when they talked about "magic."

1

And if there's anyone to blame for the shriveling death of that show's magic, it's me.

⌘

Jesus, I don't write anything for years and when Tony dies, bam, I'm sitting at his old computer typing about David Findley. David Fucking Findley, who wasn't even really David Fucking Findley.

⌘

Not that we felt magical making Acres of Perhaps. The question for every episode wasn't whether it was good but whether it was Monday: that's when we had to have the cans shipped off to the network for broadcast. The money men at the studio had no idea whether what we did was good or not, but they gave Hugh a lot of freedom because they sure didn't want to run anything valuable at 11:30 at night. As long as medicated powders and furniture polish kept flying off the shelves, we could have shown a half hour of fireflies knocking around in a jar for all they cared.

We came close.

You might remember "Woodsy," an episode David not only wrote but shot himself. That's the one where the camera stays fixed on a dark patch of woods at night for the whole half hour, and after five minutes you see tiny faces watching you through the leaves grinning madly, first a couple and then many more. About ten minutes before the end, a half dozen of these little goblin people drag a man's body across the camera's field of vision, tugging it in bursts until the shoes disappear on the left side. Then something pushes the camera over. Roll credits.

Hugh almost burst a blood vessel in his neck when David came back with that one, but he'd borrowed the camera all weekend and there wasn't much else to do but send off the episode and see what happened. A whole big nothing, that's what: people watched it, wondered what the fuck was going on, and then went to bed. We got letters about it, but no more than we did for the episode about the Hitler robot.

David pulled shit like that all the time. He was the tortured genius, treated with delicacy, and he pissed me off. I was young and insecure with a cottage in Venice to pay for, and here was this guy living like Poe in a boardinghouse, writing unfilmable stories about finding dead satyrs in a Manhattan street. David never seemed to understand there was a time when the words had to hit the page and go out to a real world of people who just wanted to be entertained.

Remember the one with two Jewish teenagers learning to fly as they plunged from the Stairs of Death holding hands at Mauthausen? That was David's. There was one told from the point of view of an atomic bomb as it dropped, admiring landmarks and slowly revealing its target is Washington; that got us a visit from the FBI. We lost General Foods over the one where Abe Lincoln turns out to be the second coming of Jesus, but at least I talked them out of spreading his arms on the stage of Ford's Theater at the end.

Hugh was the big picture guy—the big exploding "gee-whiz" picture guy. He liked to hold up his hands, framing the world with his fingers and imagining it better. To him, the three-act structure of our stories was, "What the fuck? Holy shit! Oh, my God." Why anyone trusted him with money, I have no idea, but he was no help with David.

That made me the bad guy. And it wasn't like I didn't have an imagination, either: I'd written for the pulps since the forties and knew my way around a graveyard or a ray gun. But I sure

3

as hell wasn't writing scripts about two Scotsmen pulling in Nessie's corpse with hooks so the tourists would never know she was dead. It fell to me to point out what was too expensive to film (walking skyscrapers in a city of the future) or too skull-cracked crazy (octopus women driving walking skyscrapers in a city of the future). I had to make the characters sound like real people, too, not all breathlessly eloquent.

Hugh appreciated that, I guess, the balance between us. Maybe David did, too. Thinking back on it, I was the only one with the problem.

David was so much younger than I was, very young, and he carried around an old-fashioned carpet bag with clothes and a portable typewriter, ready to sleep or write anywhere. I had no idea where he got the little money he had—God knows it wasn't rolling in from Hugh—but he spent it cracking up a car at least once a year and buying girls drinks at the Brown Derby. Hugh and I once had to bail him out of jail because he woke up inside an empty water tower.

He was six years too early for the world, born for bell bottoms and LSD. I was six years too late with my crew cut and horn-rimmed glasses. It's taken me a half century to admit this, but yeah, he was everything I didn't know I wanted to be. We were friends the way television writers are, smiling like sharks at each other across a dinner table.

4

⌘

I'm grateful to Hugh and David for at least one thing, sharks though they were: never seeming to care Tony and I were together. That meant a lot in the days when it was dangerous for two men to get a hotel room, when a neighbor peeved about too much noise could call the cops to report something worse.

Yes, they sometimes cracked jokes about where one applied to be a "confirmed bachelor," but they liked Tony. They liked the sandwiches he'd make on poker nights, not little triangles with the crusts cut off but giant heroes.

They didn't like that he was unbeatable at cards.

"Please," Hugh said once, "make an expression of any kind. Look down at your cards and then up at us."

Tony shook his head and then drew his hand down in front of his face like a curtain.

"Buddy,"–that was what Tony said in public instead of 'honey'– "With guys like us, it's all poker face."

⌘

We were mid-way through filming episodes for the second season when the Mullard family came looking for David at the studio. He didn't often show up even when the story was his, but when it wasn't, he was usually sleeping off a drunk or reading about ancient Egyptians in the library or doing some other goddamned thing.

We were working on the episode "The Dreams Come By Here Regular." I'm sure you remember it; it starred that child actress, what's-her-name, and she gets lost in the woods to be rescued by the ghosts of escaped slaves. It was all moralistic Hugh, right down to the fading strains of spirituals at the end— pretty gutsy for 1962, though, when people were getting their skulls cracked open for thinking those things in the South.

The stage was all set up as a forest at night where the action took place, and our guys were good at building forests. The trunks were huge and roughly coated, and the branches drooped with nets of fake Spanish moss. Hugh and I were looking over the script when a beam of glaring California light crawled our way across the stage.

"Close the goddamned door!" the cameraman shouted.

Figure after figure stepped in through the light, and they wove their way through our trees like pygmies coming for us in the jungle. If we'd turned the cameras on, we could have gotten an eerie scene, and I'm sure Hugh regretted it later.

A stern matron in a graying beehive came out first, clutching a patent-leather pocketbook with both hands. She examined our faces in the dim illumination behind the equipment, squinting at us each in turn.

"What can we do for you?" Hugh asked.

She didn't answer, only squaring off with him as though ready for an honest-to-God fistfight. A fistfight, by the way, that you could see she had no plans to lose.

Before it came to that, the most beautiful woman I'd ever seen came out from the fake woods behind her. She was a strawberry blonde, and she had all the grace and delicacy the old lady didn't—that most ladies didn't. Her calm eyes and strong brows, though, gave the impression that she'd learned the lady-like art of making things happen with leverage from the sides of life.

But that's David talk.

"Hello, gentlemen," the woman said, surprisingly at us. "We're looking for Leroy Dutton."

Hugh glanced around. "Any of you call yourself Leroy?"

The grips, the cable jockeys, the flannel-shirted union men who seemed to be paid to drink our coffee all froze, perhaps contemplating if it would be worth pretending to be Leroy for that pretty girl...and that awful woman. Nobody spoke up.

By then, the rest of the clan had come through—a father in a loose too-short tie, a couple of strapping brothers in coveralls, and a kid sister with cat-eye glasses. They could have been the cast of a variety show a few stages over, something wholesome sponsored by a bread company with square dancing. All they needed were straw hats.

"No Leroy here, I'm afraid," Hugh said.

The older lady snapped open her pocketbook and handed him a photograph. "He might not be calling himself Leroy anymore."

I looked over Hugh's shoulder. It was a wedding portrait, and the beauty on our stage was the bride, gazing up at her groom and holding a bouquet of wildflowers between them. The groom, of course, was David.

"This was taken three years ago," she said. "Before Leroy up and left our Melody. Not much before, let me tell you. Weeks. Right after he came back from the woods."

"He's a writer," Melody explained, as though we wouldn't know.

"He calls himself a writer," the old lady corrected. "He's a husband and a son-in-law and an employee of the J.W. Mullard Feed Company is what he is."

A husband and a son and an employee—none were things I'd ever have linked to David Findley. I mean, everyone working on that show was unemployable. We'd been too blind or flatfooted or gay to go to Korea. Some of us had dabbled in college, but those days were cut short by a few bad creative writing classes and a lack of money. We worked as clerks, as janitors, as too-old newspaper boys. And we worked on our writing, of course, holding the few checks that came in just long enough to clear before taking everyone else out for booze. We had mortgages; David had a trunk full of paperbacks. He could jump into a borrowed convertible with a cocktail waitress and go racing in the desert at three in the morning.

Though apparently he couldn't after all.

Hugh was smooth. "Doesn't look familiar to me, and I know almost every writer in this town. What about you, Barry?"

I swallowed hard and looked at the picture. "I don't think I've seen him before."

The old lady wasn't buying it, and I'm not sure Melody was either.

"Oh," Melody said, curling one side of her lips in thought. "Is there another show like this one? With little spacemen and ghosts and things?"

Hugh put his hands on his hips. "Is there another show like this one? Ma'am, this is the most inventive television program in the history of the medium. Is there—"

I cut him off before he dug any deeper. "What he means to say is that there are shows passingly similar to this one, and your husband could work for any of those. General Mills Playhouse, The Witching Hour, Dr. Hyde's Nightly Ride...maybe they're worth a try."

"They're not as good as we are," Hugh couldn't resist saying.

Melody considered this. "Well, he'd only work for the best. If he hasn't come here yet, he will. Can you tell him I'm looking for him?"

"Sure thing," I said.

"And that I love him?"

"Of course."

"And that I'll always know who he really is?"

Hugh thought a second before saying, "Okay."

The old lady pointed at Hugh. "You'd better be careful when you see him. He can take on any form."

"Believe me, lady, I know the type," Hugh said.

The family turned and headed back for the door one by one. The littlest Mullard sibling, the girl with the glasses, waited until last and handed us each something out of the pocket of her sweater: crosses fashioned from Popsicle sticks.

"In case he comes at night," she said. Then she followed her family out through our woods and into the sunshine.

Hugh shook his head and tossed his Popsicle cross to a grip. "Can we get some footage shot today?" he barked.

⌘

Tony, by the way, was not religious, which is one of about ten thousand things I liked about him. It would have been hard to be in those years, living like we were. The only place to feel and think differently than everyone else was on silly spaceman shows like Acres of Perhaps...shows you watched with thousands of other people alone in the dark.

⌘

We found David where we usually did when he wasn't at the studio: hunched in a booth at the Derby typing away on the portable with a glass of something clear and poisonous by his side. Hugh slid onto one seat and I slid onto the other right next to David.

"So, Leroy, tell us about Melody," I said.

He paused with his fingers above the keys but then plunged them down again almost in a chord to finish the sentence. He batted the carriage lever and sent it clunking to the far side.

9

"Melody," he said, "is the most beautiful and brilliant woman in the world, and I don't want to even think about your eyes on her."

"Well, everybody at the studio had eyes on her today," I said. "She came looking for you."

"Brought her whole clan," Hugh added.

"Probably spelled with a K," I said.

David tapped a Chesterfield from a pack and lit it. There was a shimmy in his hands. "That so?" he said.

"That's so," I said. I gave him time to take a drag and let out a whisper of smoke, maybe think of something to say next. When he said nothing, I did instead.

"So tell us how your marriage in a hick town crushed your artistic sensibilities until you had to break free, please. I'd like to hear it for the hundredth time, and I'll bet your version is the best."

"I didn't want to leave her. I had to."

I leaned back from the table. "You had to."

He waved his cigarette near his face. "Look, I didn't want to end up here, for Christ's sake. I'm from Jenkins Notch, North Carolina, and I spent my first twenty years thinking I'd be right happy working in a farmer's store until I could afford a place of my own. I'm a hick, whatever you assholes think, and I'm not here because I want to be famous or rich. Shit, look at you guys."

The waitress was sliding a gin and tonic over to Hugh, who came here so often he didn't have to order it.

"Writing is your job. You talk about it, think about it, work out ways to do it better. I want to get rid of it."

I said, "Yes, it's a bitch to be a genius. We get it."

"No, you don't. I'd go home with Melody right now if she was here. If I could."

"Nothing's stopping you," I said. "Except maybe an aversion to decency."

"It wasn't like that," David said. "I liked living there. I loved living with her. We were like limbs of the same tree growing back together after a fire. Even her sweat smelled good, you know? I'd come home and she'd be flushed from walking back from the school house where she taught and she'd have this scent of...the whole earth, really. Like a creek smells in the summer, or firewood in the winter."

That was eerily and terrifyingly sweet for him to say. This was a man who'd written a script about how every Mercury rocket runs on mulched pixies for fuel, after all.

"I didn't used to drink when I lived back there." His twang had come back and he sounded possessed by himself. "But there was this family—probably still is—called the McDantrys and they made moonshine out in the woods. They sold it in town from their truck, and some idiot got some for Melody and me for a wedding present."

"Something borrowed, something blue, something toxic..." I started before trailing off.

"And one night she and I are in the new house and we're rough-housing and laughing and she gets it into her head to try the stuff. 'Nobody here but us chickens,' she says, taking the Mason jar off the top shelf of the pantry and twisting off the cap. The fumes distorted her face right before she took a big pull from it, and then she handed it to me."

"So what are you going to do? Let her unman you?" Hugh asked.

11

"Right. I woke up the next morning in a rocking chair with a fawn licking from the streak of vomit down the front of my shirt. All the windows of the house were broken. Inside, I hear this sobbing."

He lit another cigarette and exhaled from his mouth.

"I go in, and sure enough, there's Melody all beat up, her face puffy and bulging like a rotten plum. She's crying and I try to console her, but she hides behind the kitchen table and won't let me near her. I'm all looking down at my hands and I want to cut them off.

"But I'm still not thinking clearly enough, so I stagger off to the woods to find the McDantrys. They sold bad stuff, right? I could have fucking killed someone. And if I still had it in me, I might as well let them have a little."

By then in David's story, Hugh had gotten this look on his face that he wanted to write this down in case it got good. I'll admit I wasn't thinking much differently myself. Hell, we could use the forest set we'd already built.

But then the story got strange even by our standards.

"Out back of the Mullard property was a swamp of pines and cypress trees stretching for miles. The ground there is blackened mud and the canopy is all grown together. The McDantrys had put planks across the cypress knees so you'd walk on this tottering path zigging and zagging through the woods. Some were slick with mold so I had to be careful, but I followed them as far as they went—a long damned way.

"It got as dark as dusk back there and it wouldn't have been hard to lose your sense of time. So it might have been an hour or even three until I came upon a big rotten cypress stump the folks around there called the Old Knot. When I say 'big,' I mean easily the size of a bus, hollowed in the middle like a bottomless well.

"There was a still there all right, camouflaged with broken branches. I was tempted to kick it off into the pit but, frankly, I'd have preferred to do that to the McDantrys.

"Of course, none were there. So I set about to wait. I walked around on the planks a bit, holding out my arms to keep my balance. I fiddled with the still to see how it worked. And then I leaned over and looked down into the stump."

"What did you see?" Hugh asked.

"I didn't see anything," David said. "It was dark. But I heard a hollow whistle, a little like the Knot was breathing—like it was the mouth of some wooden giant asleep under a blanket of mud. I reached my hand over the middle and the breeze was cool and rhythmic."

The waitress set a beer in front of me and I flinched.

"The weirdest thing was that when I shifted my weight on the board and it let out a squeal, the breeze stopped. Like something was holding its breath for me. And I wanted badly for it to start again—like when a friend jumps into a quarry pond and doesn't come up in what seems like forever?

"'Hey,' I shouted, but there was no answer.

"I got this idea I had to climb down there no matter how far it went, had to squeeze its heart with both my arms to start it again. That was crazy—for all I knew, it was a nest of rattlesnakes.

"But standing there thinking it over, I was okay with that. What else did anybody need me for? The least I could do was make Melody a happy widow instead of a miserable wife.

"So I leaned and leaned like a coward until gravity made the decision for me."

13

"Jesus," Hugh said.

"I fell for a long, long time—so long that I had dreams. The vibration of cold whispers on my ears. The tremble of fingers up and down my arms. Something with claws combing over my scalp. I smelled oceans from other places, imagined music played with water and leaves."

Bullshit, I thought...but didn't say.

"And then I hit the ground. Or so I figured. I woke up flat on my face in my own front yard. Melody came running out and kissed me and said we'd never talk about it again and it wasn't my fault and she'd still love me forever."

Here he paused.

"Well, a funny thing occurred to me that night, naked with our sweat soaked into the sheets and our scents on each other's lips. What if this was the bottom of the Old Knot, with a different Melody and a different house and a different town? What if up there somewhere was a woman still scared of me? And why wasn't this one?"

Leave it to David Findley, or Leroy Whatever, to have the world's most sublime and esoteric drinking blackout.

"After, I had weird dreams of what was going on here or up there, and I noticed things didn't always connect. I'd think I'd said something here but really I'd said it in a dream up top of the Old Knot, or I'd lose a day in one place or the other. Folks got nervous around me because I'd stare off somewhere and then write down what I could in a notebook I got from the dime store. When that wasn't fast enough, I got the typewriter."

"So why'd you leave?" Hugh asked.

"Melody wasn't worried at first when I clattered away in the kitchen with a board balanced on the arms of a chair. But then I stopped sleeping and going to work. I stopped leaving the

14

house and shaving. I stopped talking, stopped focusing on anything in front of me. She called over my folks to talk sense to me. Reverend Pritchett stopped by. And when I heard them talking about "getting me out," I decided I'd better get myself out first. I packed up one night and lit out west. And the only thing I can make or sell is...whatever that fall gave me."

David drank the rest of his liquor in one long swallow. You'd think he'd have learned not to do that from his own story.

And that's what it was: a story. A good one, like all of his, but a tall tale myth meant to make him seem like the Paul Bunyan of weird fiction or something.

"So you drank bad moonshine, beat up your wife while barely conscious, stumbled into the woods, and got a concussion after falling into an old tree stump?" I said.

David eyed me calmly. "Yeah, if you think so."

"One of those McDantry people dragged you back home where you came to, and ever since, you've suffered the lingering effects of your concussion, plus some uncharacteristic guilt. Mystery solved."

"If you say so," he said.

Hugh, not helping, asked, "So there are different versions of us back where you came from?"

"Yeah," David said. "Barry here is writing for the Saturday Evening Post."

Hugh and I stared and he let us dangle a moment before laughing.

"Barry, I have no idea if you even exist, here or there. I'm not sure I'm creative enough to invent you or Hugh. Or, shit, all of Hollywood. Who would imagine the studio system? Jesus, I hope not me."

15

Then, being writers, we spent the night getting drunk and bitching about the money men.

⌘

You know, Tony and I never got to speed around the desert in a Karmann Ghia convertible like David did with his girlfriends. We could never fight in public with me chasing him out of a restaurant to apologize, either, or walk close on the pier. We lived in a closet built for two for fifty years, and when I finally found the guts to step out, he was too sick to step out with me.

⌘

The saying goes that to be great is to be misunderstood, and most people assume this also means that to be misunderstood is to be great. But there are lots of misunderstood people who are a long way from greatness.

When I crawled into my bed beside Tony's that night, I wondered which one David "Leroy" Findley was: a visionary or some delusional hick good at sounding like one. Or maybe there wasn't a difference.

What did "Woodsy" even mean when you thought about it? Anybody can film random movements and rely on the viewers' perceptions to make it art, but unless it says something, what's the damned point? Acres of Perhaps wasn't in the "giving-voice-to-David's-demons" business; it was in the "entertaining-and-enlightening" one. We made people think about race, nostalgia, paranoia...not the stitching of the universe. Someone could create the Clorox Kafka Hour for that.

Tony rolled over under his sheets to face me. We'd just moved to this Craftsman bungalow in Venice then and air conditioning was a science fictional concept to us. Even a fan was something that cost money, and so he slept without much on at all. I remember this now only because, well, I thought right then that Tony was as good as Melody any day of the week.

I told him what had happened, about the Mullard family and David's secret identity, about how the whole genius act had a clichéd story behind it except for the falling into the netherworld part which was pure delusion. He listened with his head propped up in his hand under the moonlight, asking questions and nodding at the answers.

At the end, he asked, "So what is he going to do?"

David had ducked the question at the Derby so I could only offer my guess. "He'll probably keep avoiding her until she gives up and goes home."

He considered a moment. "You sound angry about it."

"I don't think angry is the right word. Annoyed. I'm annoyed things are easier for him because he has people like Hugh and Melody and me carrying his load of the ordinary."

"You know what I think?" That was one of my favorite phrases of his; it was like a motor revving. "Men like David make women into muses so they have someone to blame when they don't deliver the goods. And they make women into anti-muses, too."

"Anti-muses."

"Yeah. Like this poor Melody. She's the boat anchor mooring him to reality, right? So he builds it all up until she seems to be after his soul, and then he's justified in leaving her."

Tony was a part-time illustrator for magazines in L.A. and San Francisco, and he had a way of drawing exactly what you needed to see but no more. He sometimes did it with words, too.

17

"Do you think I'm that way?"

He smiled and reached for my hands. "You don't have a muse, love. In the same way astronauts and carpenters don't. You just do things."

Tony never misunderstood me, and sometimes that was consolation enough for not being great.

I'd leaned in closer when there came a thunder of fists against the front door.

Tony sighed and gathered up the blankets around him. Then he reached for his cigarettes and said, "Better go see what David wants."

"What makes you think it's David?"

He tapped the end of the pack. "It's the way his life works."

I pulled on an undershirt over my pajama pants and headed for the door. A shadowed head bobbed in the window, and I could tell from the wild spray of hair that it really was David.

"What do you want?" I asked through the door.

"Barry! You've got to let me in. They're after me."

"Who?"

"Melody and her folks!"

I imagined them walking down the street with torches and pitchforks, and I'll admit I liked the image.

"Where are they?"

"They're here," he cried, twisting the door knob and thumping himself against it.

I opened the door and he stumbled inside. He tried his best to slam it again but I was holding it.

"This is silly," I said. "They're people. Be with her, don't be with her—just tell her the truth."

Out in the darkened street, I saw the Mullard family walking abreast in a single line, patrolling with flashlights like you would if searching for a lost dog. They pivoted as one group at the end of my driveway and marched toward us.

"Okay," I said, closing the door.

David did me the courtesy of bolting it shut. He reached for a chair to prop under it but I stopped him.

I watched through the window as the Mullards formed an arc around the entrance to my house like Christmas carolers. Melody left the group and knocked gently.

"Mr. Weyrich? I think Leroy is inside your house. Can he come out so we can talk to him?"

"Hold on a moment," I yelled. Then, turning to David, I whispered, "What do you expect me to do?"

"Tell them to go away. Tell them you're calling the cops."

"Mr. Weyrich?" This time it was the mother. "That's my daughter's lawful husband in there."

David shook his head but I leaned closer to the window. "Look, I don't want to be involved in this at all. Maybe everybody should call it a night, get some sleep, and then get together somewhere tomorrow to talk it all over."

The Mullards closed in.

"Hey, Tony," David said.

Tony was leaning in the hallway in his navy-blue pajamas. He lowered his cigarette from his lips and said, "Hello, David."

"You've got to talk some sense into her, Tony."

He arched an eyebrow. "Why me?"

"Because you have feelings and things," David said quickly, still peering through the window.

I watched as the two brothers broke off from the group and out of my vision. I wondered if I'd remembered to lock the back door. Then I wondered if it wouldn't be just as well for these

19

guys to carry David out of my house and my life. Maybe I could hurry and unlock it.

Tony came closer. "Melody, honey?"

"Yes," was the quiet response.

"My name is Tony. I'm Barry's roommate."

Isn't that funny how quickly it ran off his tongue? He didn't even have to pause anymore.

"David—Leroy—isn't in a condition to talk to you right now."

"Has he changed form?"

Tony turned to David; he'd sat down in one of our living room chairs and was squeezing his temples with his palms.

"No, he's still Leroy," Tony said.

On the other side of the house, the back-door knob rattled. Then a giant rhomboid head with speckled stubble craned in through the open kitchen window. He peered around, looking down at the sink and up at the ceiling, maybe judging if there was room to climb through.

"Hey," I said, stepping over to the sink. I picked up the fancy new water sprayer gizmo and gave him a quick spritz in the face. He retreated sputtering and I slammed the window closed.

By now, David was holding his head in his hands, covering his eyes.

"Who the hell are these people?" I said.

"They think I'm possessed by the devil," he said quietly.

"So do I, but you don't see me climbing into people's houses to get you."

"They found me at the boardinghouse, I have no idea how. Melody's always been able to find me wherever I was like she can feel me, a phantom limb."

I wondered if Tony could. Probably, knowing him.

"Do you have anything to drink?" David asked.

"For you, no," Tony said. "You smell like a gas tank."

"It's how I listen," he said.

Outside, the Mullards began to sing. They weren't bad acapella, but when the little one started in on the banjo, it was beautiful. Beautiful and scary because, Jesus, who carries around a goddamned banjo?

I glowered at David with my arms folded. "Your whole life is one long episode of *Acres of Perhaps*, isn't it?"

So began a strange siege, me sitting on the couch keeping an eye on the Mullards through the blinds and Tony sitting in the other recliner watching David. The Mullards sang hymns in low voices while David muttered to himself with his hands clawed into the arms of my chair like an astronaut going up.

"This is ridiculous," I whispered to Tony. I probably didn't have to.

"Maybe everybody will get tired and go home," he said.

"We are home," I said.

Not long after, a rancid odor overtook the room. It took me a moment to realize what it was: David, head lolled back and his mouth wide open, had pissed himself in my favorite chair.

Tony figured it out at the same time. "It's not like that chair was cheap," he said.

I grabbed David by his shirt and yanked him up. A dark spot had bloomed on his pants.

"David, wake up!"

He rolled his head to one side and then the other, mumbling. The words were faint and garbled at first but then they resolved like a radio bearing in on the right station.

"What if people make cities itch?" he said.

21

"Jesus Christ," I said. "'Antelope umbrellas crying in the wind.' There. I'm a genius, too."

"You're the one who thinks it's magic."

"People who piss themselves in my house don't get to ever use that word around me again."

He tilted his head back way farther than I thought possible, opened his mouth like the tall front doors of a church, and let out a long, low wail. Then he pivoted his head forward again and said, "Where's my typewriter?"

I glanced around in case he'd brought it inside. When I didn't see it, I opened the blinds and squinted on the porch. There was his black case sitting amongst the Mullards.

"You really want it?"

"Barry," Tony said in his admonishing voice.

"Yes," David said. "I've got to get this down."

"Excellent," I said. I turned the deadbolt on the door.

"Are you sure you want to do that?" Tony asked.

"Never surer," I said, opening it.

The Mullards all stood from where they were sitting on the low adobe wall, looks of surprise on their faces.

"He's all yours," I said, shoving him into their arms.

The two beefy brothers caught him while the mother looked down with disgust. She'd probably have let him hit the cement face first.

"It's okay," Melody said, her hands on the side of his face.

"No, it isn't," David groaned.

"Peace be with you, praise the Lord, whatever the fuck," I said, holding up my hand jauntily and then slamming the door.

"Hugh's going to kill you," Tony said.

"No, he's not," I said absently, watching through the blinds as the Mullard brothers hoisted David on their shoulders like a trophy deer. "Jesus is cheaper than detox."

They'd left David's typewriter behind and, well, you can't leave something like that lying around. I reached out and grabbed it.

⌘

David was a drunk, an eloquent drunk, and it was hard to blame him because hey, you've got to do whatever makes you brave. For some people that's booze, for others it's drugs, for other still it's narcissism or vengeance or desperation. I don't know what made it possible for me to face the page, but keeping stupid words like "magic" out of my head probably helped, telling myself it was like making a chair or a sandwich instead of something alive.

⌘

It's not what you think, that I jumped on a chance to take out a rival. After that night, my frustrations with David turned to pity. He happened to be sick in a way that helped him write stories for our television show, but it wasn't comfortable for him. It hurt him to do. It might even have killed him one day.

But first, as Tony predicted, Hugh wanted to kill me.

"'Jesus is cheaper than detox'? That's what you have to say?" he told me at the studio the next day. "People come back from detox, Barry."

"He'll come back. They might not even get him all the way to Jenkins Notch. We're going to get a collect call from a Howard Johnson's in Kansas after he escapes, and we'll go pick him up. But you know what? He'll damned well be sober."

23

"You understand he's the engine of this whole show, don't you?"

"Well, I like to think I'm useful, too."

Hugh brandished his clipboard over his head. "You're the brakes! You're the rearview mirror!"

"Okay, well, fuck you. But listen. David drunk would last what, another season? At the most."

"You don't know that!"

"At the most. Then he'd wrap himself around a tree or hang himself by his belt in a closet. You know how many scripts he'd write then? Zero."

"They're going to make him into a revivalist preacher."

Okay, I smiled a little to imagine old Leroy Dutton swinging a Bible over his head on a plywood stage somewhere, sweat staining the armpits of his short-sleeved buttoned shirt. He'd be good at it, I thought. Quick on his feet, anyway.

"Look," I said. "he's a married man. He has a wife and responsibilities and we shouldn't interfere with that just because you think he's the only way to make a television show."

"Married man?" Hugh said. "What the hell do you know about being married?"

I used to think Hugh only meant about thirty percent of what he said, less when he was angry, but it was funny how even irrational, he still remembered where to hit me.

I was considering where to hit him back when the stage door opened again and for the second time in as many days, Melody Mullard Dutton was walking through our woods. She was by herself this time, thankfully.

"There's something wrong with David," she said.

"Of course there is," I said.

⌘

You know what Tony did every morning for fifty years? He'd open the office curtains facing out to the street, tying them neatly to the side. He'd straighten papers on the desk. He'd set down a cup of coffee he'd brewed on the stove, the way he knew I liked it best. He'd turn on the typewriter.

And because he did, I sat down every day. Sometimes I'd peck something out but mostly I didn't.

⌘

David had escaped, though he was hardly on the lam: he jumped out of the Mullards' 1940 DeSoto at the intersection of Wilshire and LaBrea on the way out of town, and now they were pretty sure he was holed up at the Derby. It says all you need to know about Hugh that he was relieved a beautiful woman and her good Christian family had failed to lure his writer to a wholesome life in Jenkins Notch.

"He knows where his home is," Hugh said later. "Not shuffling barefoot with a bunch of Snuffy Smith castoffs."

The only thing keeping the Mullard boys from storming into the Derby and carrying David out on their shoulders like a sack of grain was that Melody had a plan. In Hugh's office with her hands folding and unfolding in her lap, she explained it to us.

"Leroy thinks he's fallen through that old stump and he's now living on the other side, right?"

I had doubts he thought so literally, but I nodded with Hugh.

"When she taught me how to sew, Mawmaw,"—I think that's what she called her, and it made me think of a giant double mouth lined with sharp teeth— "told me that sometimes

25

the only way to undo a knot is to push the needle back through it."

"Okay," I said, pinching the bridge of my nose. "I think we might be getting a bit too literal here."

"So you want to push him back through the Knot again?" Hugh asked.

"Yes," she said.

"That still doesn't solve the problem of getting him back to North Carolina in the first place, does it?" I asked.

"We wouldn't have to if there was a forest here."

Of course, there happened to be the perfect forest not forty feet from us. A week earlier and the stage would have been New York City. A week later and it would be acting as Moon Base Theta. The Mullards had shown up right in the middle of our very own North Carolina backwoods, almost as though it was destiny.

"All it needs is a Knot," she added. "Or something he thinks is one."

I watched Hugh's eyebrows lift in excitement as they did before any new production, when the budget shortfalls and actor disagreements and special effects problems hadn't started yet. If there was ever a man born to build a fake portal between worlds to convince a half-mad, half-drunk genius he was sane again...it was Hugh Kline.

26

The question, though, was why he'd want to do it, aside from the artistic challenge. As he leaned across his desk with a pencil and paper so Melody could sketch the stump, I wondered what his angle could be. When he glanced at me and grinned, I knew it for sure.

The Mullards wanted an exorcism. They assumed a sober, demon-free Leroy Dutton would climb out of that stump all blinking in the light of Jesus to return to Jenkins Notch. Hugh, on the other hand, assumed David Findley would climb out, look around at his crazy hick relatives and then never leave Los Angeles again. He wasn't exorcising the Devil. He was exorcizing the Mullards.

"If there's one thing I've learned about working with writers, it's to meet them on their own level," he told me after Melody was gone.

"What's my level?" I asked.

"You don't have a level, Barry. That's why I like you."

And hearing that—knowing it—solidified which fate I wanted for David Findley.

⌘

It's not like I never wrote again after the show went under. I moved on to comedies and little dramas to keep food on the table, not because I was gifted at it but because I showed up and produced words when they needed them. In Hollywood, that beats genius every time.

I never knew why guys like David Findley got all the credit for creativity. Anyone can wave his hands and yell, "Magic dust!" or "interdimensional tree stump" to explain everything away.

⌘

We left the set decorator to build the stump while we went to fetch David. He'd slipped away from the Derby by the time we got there, and we checked two bars before finding him again. I don't remember the place, but I do remember him sitting under the only bright light in the room, writing in a goddamned steno pad with an arc of empty glasses around it.

"Do we grab him or what?" I asked Hugh.

27

"No, let's try this," Hugh said, hunching a little toward the back as though he was trying to go unnoticed.

When David looked up, I could see his eyes weren't quite focusing on us, and the writing on his pad couldn't be decipherable even to him.

"We got rid of them," Hugh whispered.

We sat down on the other side of the table.

"How?" David asked, his voice hoarse.

"Told them you'd gone to the desert to think things through," Hugh said. "They'll be there for another four hours, easy."

David glanced down at the steno pad. "Thanks. I appreciate it. I need some room—"

"What you need," I said, holding up a hand for a waitress or a bartender or whatever worked in that hole of a bar, "is a celebratory drink."

"We all do," Hugh said.

"Yeah, we do," David said, dreamily.

So that was the plan. We let David drink as much as he wanted, "slaking the demon" as the Mullards would have called it, matching him with one drink of ours for three of his. We figured he'd get drunk enough to drag back to the studio for his exorcism in about two hours.

It took more like four and the cost of at least one episode to get him to the blubbering mess we required. He descended to that state in layers: first he was sentimental, then he was funny, and finally he was full of strange advice.

"You know how you can be as good a writer as I am, Barry?" he asked.

"Please tell me," I said. By then, I was barely keeping my own liquor down in my stomach where it belonged.

"By not imagining I'm a better writer than you are," he said.

"That's deep. You're like some alcoholic Confucius."

When David started to drizzle down his seat toward the floor, we figured it was time to get him home. I caught him before his head hit the carpet.

"Jesus," Hugh said. "Maybe we ought to take him to the hospital instead."

"We're taking him to a spiritual one." I ducked beneath one of David's arms. "Come on, lift the other side."

We got David into the car. We got the car across town. We got the car through the studio gate. We got David up, out, and onto his spongey feet. We got him out of the California sun and into the North Carolina backwoods in the time it took to write this paragraph.

It set was the best we'd ever built. I felt the warmth in those woods, the Southern stickiness of them. I smelled the moss. I heard the cicadas. I saw, yes, the winding path of planks leading off into the swamp.

Standing at the end closest to us was Melody.

"We're here to take you home, baby," she said, reaching for David. "We came through the Knot."

He turned into my chest and made a few sloppy skids on the stage to get away. "Get out of here! This place isn't for you!"

"It isn't for you, either," she said calmly.

"Come on, buddy," I said.

Hugh followed us on the creaking path deep into the soundstage. I hadn't realized it was that big. Helping David along those planks, I felt the danger of falling into the muck, of stirring up snakes. I felt the trees watching me.

We came to the stump—the Knot—in only a few minutes but it seemed much longer. They'd outdone themselves with

29

lumber and plaster: it was giant and creepy and it cost as much as three episodes we'd now have to film on canned sets in the backlot. But you could park a Volkswagen inside if you wanted to. The set decorator must have gotten it right because David recoiled when we got there.

"We're going home," Melody said like a beckoning spirit, a dryad or a nymph, her hand dipping gracefully from her pale wrist.

We propped David up near the edge. I peered down into the stump and saw the stage hands had lined the bottom with black cloth—a kind of hammock. It would catch him when he fell.

If he fell. He clutched the stump and wouldn't even look inside. "I can't go," he said.

Melody steered herself into his vision. "Baby, listen to me. We're going home now. You're going to remember this all like a dream because that's what it is."

"I can't take it back with me," he said.

It was growing clear that we'd soon have to toss him into the stump by force unless someone thought of the right thing to say. Everybody turned to me.

It wasn't a rational decision, what I said next. It came as some awful belch of the id.

"There is no 'it,' Leroy," I said.

He closed his eyes as though that would close his ears.

"Nothing's talking to you or through you. You write weird stuff and what does it change? Nothing. Somebody sits up late at night watching our fucking show in an undershirt with a bottle of beer in his hand. His eyes get opened to the dark truths of the universe. But then he crawls off to bed and gets up the next morning for work. He farts in the elevator, he looks down a lady's dress...it's all gone."

David didn't say anything, but he did slump farther against the Knot.

"Even if you had something, people would just flush it down the toilet. It's good they flush it down the toilet because how else are they supposed to sell insurance or sweep floors or wipe baby asses after knowing all of that? It's a defense mechanism."

Hugh's smile faded. "Hey," he said.

"It's selfish when you think about it," I pressed. "Shoving people's faces in lives they'll never have, things they'll never feel that you made up out of nowhere."

"Selfish?"

"Yeah. That's what it seems to me. You're not supposed to see that stuff and you sure as hell aren't supposed to make us see it, either."

"I don't—"

It takes a writer to know how to demolish another writer. And with Melody looking on and her family all praying, I did it.

"Go home, Leroy. Go the fuck home. This world is lost. The one on your side of the Knot, though? Maybe it isn't. Maybe you'll give your magic to your kids. Maybe you'll just live."

David's voice cracked when he said, "What if I don't see anymore? What if I can only see here?"

"Then it wasn't yours to see in the first place," I said.

The little Mullard girl began to sing. Melody's brothers joined in as the harmony and soon the whole family had clasped hands in a circle around Hugh's fake stump.

31

David turned his back to me on his hands and knees and I wondered what he was doing. Then he put one wobbling hand on the edge of the stump followed by the other, and he pushed himself slowly to his feet.

"Hey," Hugh said again, pushing me away. "You do see things, and you need to share them with people who don't."

David closed his eyes and swayed a moment.

"No, I don't," he said quietly. "I'm not one of the good guys."

Melody came up smiling with one hand held out for him.

"Walk with me again until you are?" she said.

He took her hand with the wide eyes and open mouth of a man being saved at the last second from drowning in the sea. Together they stepped onto the edge. They paused and gazed at each other like the wedding picture. This was another one, a renewal of the vows.

"Do you want to say goodbye?" she asked him.

He glanced over at Hugh and I. Hugh was reaching for him with a look of feral desperation on his face. Me, I nodded to David and he nodded back.

"No," he said. "Never again."

Then she took him into her arms in a dancing embrace and they plunged into the Knot. I half expected them to disappear in a flash. Or maybe I hoped.

All I heard was the pop and creak of them hitting canvas. When we approached, she was cradling him close like an infant and he was unconscious.

The Mullards came forward with a blanket and they bundled David inside. The brothers hoisted him between them and started for the studio door.

"Thank you all," Melody said, clasping mine and Hugh's hands. "You saved a life today."

Hugh tugged his away. "No, we murdered a great show that made people happy." He turned to me. "You murdered it."

I didn't think so then, not yet, so I didn't even watch as he stormed off through the forest, punching tree after tree.

"I'm glad we could help," I said.

Melody kissed me on the cheek and hurried off after the limp form of her husband, the late David Findley.

⌘

Tony wasn't well enough to travel in person at the end thanks to the cancer growing in his body like something on one of our old shows. I tried last October to rent a Winnebago and take him up the coast; he always loved the trees like David. We got maybe thirty miles out before he was too sick to keep going, but it wasn't him who said it. He'd have gone the whole way in that little plastic bathroom to make me feel better.

Make me feel better.

What he did instead with the last year he had was walk the world through Google Maps, steering down back country roads with the arrow keys. He went twice or three times across the country that way.

⌘

I told myself *Acres of Perhaps* died for many reasons, not just because of losing our resident "genius." People gave a lot less of a shit about fantasy and a lot more about the bullet-flying, hose-spraying, billy-clubbing reality of the time. If you were square, you wanted to be told about better times on television in Westerns and variety shows. If you were cool, a show like ours couldn't keep up with the farm-league David Findleys on every college campus with speed, weed, and acid. If you wanted weird, if you wanted surreal, there was always the news.

We tried, though, and I wrote my best scripts in that last half season. Remember the one where the disgraced comic book artist has to draw pictograms for our first contact with an alien race? That was mine. I also did the one where the white-bread people of a wholesome Midwestern town chase the stranded motorcycle gang into a warehouse and burn it down.

But come on. It was over. And as the stories and scripts came slower to me, I began to realize I might be over, too. I knew it on the last day of filming when Hugh handed me my check.

"You know not to come back here, don't you?" he said.

"I sure do," I said, folding the check for my pocket.

Hugh and I made up a little before he died. We were in the elevator at a convention years later, standing in opposite corners with grinning teenagers glancing back and forth between us, when out of nowhere he said, "The fucking Love Boat? Really?"

I calmly looked at him and said, "Flood Zone Manhattan? Really?"

Deadpan, he said, "We're both writing disaster pictures."

"At least Ethel Merman dies in yours," I said.

We laughed together for as long as it took to get to the lobby, and Hugh patted my shoulder with one shaking hand on his way out. That was it. That was as close as we got.

The next year I was writing for Charles in Charge.

⌘

This is Tony's computer, and I barely know how they work. I follow the paths he made for me, click the things he showed me how to click, let him do the looking I've always been afraid to do, and I've been exploring his mind when I'm not typing this.

Yesterday, I found the orange teardrop marking a spot in the North Carolina foothills in Google Maps. It had a label, and the label was, "Go here when I die."

So I am.

⌘

Jenkins Notch is in its own valley between two ridges of the Appalachian foothills, and first you go up a road of hairpin turns and switchbacks before coming down again. Not that Tony went there in person, of course. But for him to find the town and find the farm, even when he was in too much pain to sit for twenty minutes at a time...it probably almost felt that way.

The place looks like one of our old sets, Fantasia Americana. There's a real general store where old men sit around a giant wooden spool playing checkers. There's a post office operating from an old mobile home surrounded on three sides by a handicapped ramp. They've got a Main Street, too, but the little hardware store and clothing shop have long been boarded up, and the only busy place in town is the Circle K convenience store.

I followed the line Tony drew for me off the main road and through town and into the forest and finally down a bumping dirt track with a ridge of weeds growing out from the middle. The closer I got, the more I worried about whom I would find at the end. I hadn't called ahead, and Leroy Dutton could

35

stagger from his shack with one overall strap hanging loose from a beefy shoulder and a cocked shotgun on his arm, thinking I'm the tax man. I could end this journey bleeding out in the dust with my chest turned to hamburger.

That's not the reason I didn't go to see Leroy first, though.

I'm no commando or wilderness scout, so it took me some wandering and thrashing through the brush to find my way to the low-sloping hammock of loamy soil that David described for us all those years ago. I glanced between the sycamores for the little goblin things of "Woodsy" but I didn't see any.

When I came to a path of planks, I knew I was close. I followed them deeper into what now were oaks and cypress, big trees with heavy drooping limbs. Hanging from some were unlit oil lanterns, maybe placed by Leroy himself, and there was evidence people had been walking through recently: trimmed branches, flattened leaves.

It never occurred to me that the Knot could have rotten into the ground over the fifty years since Leroy fell inside. It didn't seem possible. And when I reached a domed clearing with a single heavy beam of sunlight aimed at the center, I was not surprised to see the Knot waiting for me.

Our replica on the stage was almost perfect, but this one was even larger than I imagined. Even now, rotten down low to an irregular circle, it still felt mighty. Someone had assembled a half-circle of log benches around it.

I'd come a long way, right? I wasn't drunk or imaginative or knighted by the gods with any magical perception, but yes, I leaned over and looked down into the Knot.

It was dark, just as David had described. There was a slight intimation of a breeze, a breathing, also like he'd said. My eyes couldn't focus on the bottom, black and speckled with something like stars. It might have been night on the other side, where David Findley was still writing in an attic somewhere with a bottle of gin beside him.

Where Tony was speeding down the Pacific Coast Highway with me.

I closed my eyes and tipped myself inside.

⌘

We had a hard time agreeing on the opening credits for Acres of Perhaps. A time-lapse of day fading to night in the desert? Turning pages of a book? The sparks of a campfire winding upward to the stars? A flying saucer hovering in observation above a tranquil Earth?

Hugh wanted something I called the Flying Antique Store, old porcelain dolls and Victorian chairs and grandfather clocks tumbling at the camera from some distant point in space, probably because the props were free. David, who couldn't care less about the credits, half-heartedly suggested the ticker-tapper of a news broadcast from the "far edges of imagination," something to lure in the suburban zombies he hoped to awaken.

My idea—and I've marveled since that it came to me—was to show a family sitting down to watch television on the other side of the glass, Mom in her housecoat and Pop in his loosened tie and the kids settling in, all of them staring expectantly at the viewers as though they were about to be the show. That's what we went with.

37

I saw none of those things falling through the Knot like I expected. I would have settled for scenes from my life because at least Tony would be there, but all I got was the stretch effect

from Vertigo, zooming the edges of that stump into infinity,
lined with swimming lights.

It felt like settling into bed after being awake for years.

⌘

Tony was not the one who woke me, but I wasn't surprised. What were the chances he'd be waiting by the Knot on the other side when I came through?

The man who did was heavyset with horn-rimmed glasses and a head of white unruly hair. He wasn't in overalls and he didn't have a shotgun, just an undershirt and blue jeans.

"Barry?" he was saying.

"What year is it?" I croaked. "Who's the President? Did 9/11 still happen?"

The man who once was David Findley sat on the edge of the stump. "Tony's still gone," he said. "I'm sorry."

"Are you still Leroy Dutton?"

He clasped my arm and tugged me from the soft black soil. "Always was," he said.

With his help I got to my feet, knee-deep in leaves. I found my way back over onto solid land in three wobbling steps.

"Are you still..."

"A hillbilly? If you're asking if I can play a banjo, I have to say the answer is yes, but I can only pick out the first few bars of the *Acres of Perhaps* theme."

I peered down into the Knot and all feeling of infinite depth and darkness was gone. "So it is just a stump."

David glanced in. "I've gone back and forth on that. I've never believed like I did back then, but then, maybe I don't have to."

I felt very strange and light, and it took me a moment to ask, "How did you know? About Tony?"

"He sent a letter and told us you'd be coming."

Tony, still planning my travel from beyond the grave. "When?" I asked.

"I'd have to look at the letter," he said. "A couple of months ago. You want to come back to the house to see it, maybe get some water?"

"No moonshine?" I said.

"I quit that stuff years ago, believe me, and the McDantrys up and left in 1970 anyway. I bought their property from the bank."

"You own the Knot?"

"I own the Knot." He grinned. "Isn't that crazy?"

"Yes," I said. It all was.

"The kids and grandkids used it for a stage," Leroy said. "They did puppet shows and magic shows and little plays and Franny used to have her revival sermons here for us. She's a Unitarian minister now."

"Children played in the Knot?"

"They still do sometimes when they come to visit," Leroy said. "We built a little platform for it and set up the benches like our own Globe Theater."

"They don't...fall through?"

"Not literally, no."

By then I was feeling warm, and my head felt heavy and barely attached to my neck.

"Hey," I said, taking his arm before I fell back in. "That whole thing back then in LA...I wasn't your friend."

"I know," Leroy said.

"I killed you," I said.

39

"A little bit," he conceded.

"Stories came to you easily and love came to you easily and you could be whatever you wanted in the open and you didn't want what I couldn't have."

"I knew that fifty years ago, Barry. Did you come to hear how everything turned out okay? That's fine, but first you have to know that it didn't for a long time. For a long time, I was the world's angriest feed and seed delivery man."

"I'm sorry," I said quietly.

"You have to understand that, okay? You did something shitty to someone who saw you as a friend."

Keep going, I thought. Go all the way through with the needle, me or the Knot, I didn't care.

"But I did something you didn't. I healed and scarred over. Maybe it was easier here in the woods with Melody, but you could have done it, too, if you'd let yourself. You didn't have to write for *Diff'rent Strokes* or *The Facts of Life* or whatever you did, and you didn't have to blame me or yourself for it."

"I should have been the one who left the show," I said.

"Why? You were always as good as me. You're the one who didn't think so, only because you did it differently."

I squeezed my eyes shut with my fingers. I killed him for nothing.

"All those stories that could have been," I said.

"You still wrote some," Leroy said.

"No, I mean you. I mean your stories."

Leroy squinted at me. "Do you think I stopped writing?"

"I thought—"

"—that I'd be too busy shooting Indians and skinning raccoons? Who do you think wrote those plays and puppet shows?"

"It's not the same," I said.

"The same as what?"

"The same as *Acres of Perhaps*."

"Barry," he said. "I don't want to let you off the hook without giving you some more shit first, but what do you think I've been writing?"

"Puppet shows," I mumbled. "Plays for kids."

"It was just a different network," Leroy said. "And my grandson Tucker? He can do one hell of an impression of a dropping atomic bomb."

Wait, I wanted to say. I wanted the world to wait, let me hear it clearly. "You wrote scripts?"

Leroy shrugged. "Sure. Here and there, maybe a couple hundred."

A couple hundred. Scripts. Of *Acres of Perhaps*.

"Are you sure I'm not on the other side of the Knot?"

"If you can't tell the difference, Barry, then maybe there isn't one."

⌘

On our way back, we walked in silence until Leroy said, "You know, I could have written for The Love Boat, too."

"Could you?"

"Sure. They pull into Acapulco and at midnight, the ghosts of murdered Aztecs steal everyone's gold."

"You'd have to write in Billy Barty or Paul Lynde," I said.

"Okay. One is a famous diamond thief and the passengers hang him from a yard arm when he doesn't confess."

41

"That's not bad," I said.

⌘

We followed the planks back toward a farm, not a gray shanty with the siding peeling at the corners but something with two stories and a gleaming metal roof. A woman with gorgeous long gray hair hanging almost to her waist was climbing out of a giant Toyota pick-up truck. She was wearing a suit.

Leroy pointed to me. "Look what I found in the Knot."

She didn't close the door. She hurried over, her heels kicked free, but then she stopped with her hands on her hips.

"Are you taking him back to sin?"

"What?" I glanced at Leroy and then back to her. I never imagined she might be the one to greet me with a shotgun, probably not far out of reach in that truck. "No. No. Not at all. I wanted to—"

She pulled me in for a hug. I didn't raise my arms to return it right away, only slowly.

"It's okay, Barry. That's what my family thought. I just wanted my husband back." She leaned back, looking me over. "How long were you out there?"

"I think he might have been lurking there since the 60s," Leroy said.

She frowned but said, "Well, that would explain a lot. I'm sorry I just got home. Had to go to the school board in town."

"She used to be superintendent," Leroy said. "Still is, if you count all the 'consulting' she does."

I wondered if her district taught evolution. I had a feeling it did if Leroy was anything to go by.

"Are you going to stay awhile?" she asked me.

"Do you want me to?"

"We both do," she said. "Tony did, too."

"I'm sorry?" I said, not sure I'd heard.

"Come on," Leroy said.

We walked to the edge of the grass beneath a copse of trees toward a small shed or cabin with three lightly-molded windows. He opened the door for me and inside were two desks, one a computer and one with Leroy's old typewriter.

"Tony sent it a few months ago," Melody said. "He told us you kept it for years."

"Yeah," I said.

Leroy pointed. "What I figure is you can use that and I can use the computer, or maybe the other way around, and I can write stories about walking skyscrapers and you can write stories about Mars."

"Who would want them?" I asked.

"Well, Tony would, for one," he said. "But I'm guessing we can find some asshole in Hollywood to sell them for us."

So I'm sitting now in a creaking swivel chair. I'm looking out through the windows. There's a glass beside me of something called "unsweet tea" which is what we drink around here now instead of booze. I'm resting my fingers on the keys—I don't plan to type, don't plan to even try—but the cool plastic waits.

Waits for when I'm ready again.

S1E2: "Ourselves and Immortality"

Air Date: October 19, 1961
Writer: Hugh Kline
Director: Hugh Kline

Synopsis: Teresa (played by Helen Fischer) is obsessively in love with her neighbor Harold, who is unfortunately obsessed with something else: building a nuclear bomb shelter in his back yard. Teresa comes around often to talk as he digs and pours concrete, and she even offers advice on some feminine touches like a fake window with plastic flowers. He grunts and nods and takes her advice, but he never allows her inside.

As her desperation grows, Teresa concocts a plan to attract Harold's attention once and for all.

In the middle of a working day when their suburban neighborhood is mostly empty, she enlists the help of a tech-savvy nephew who jams the local TV signal and transmits an emergency attack warning on the radio, and her sister activates the old air raid siren at the fire station.

Harold, already on the razor's edge of paranoia, leaps from his bed and hurries to the shelter where Teresa is waiting in her nicest dress and heels. She begs to be allowed into his shelter and Harold weighs the possibility, asking how much she eats in a typical day and how fertile she is. She assures him she's very fertile but he still hesitates.

45

As they begin to argue about her suitability to the future human race, Teresa's sister and nephew run up screaming that it's a real attack and they need to get inside. Harold's still skeptical, and as he folds his arms declaring there's only room for him, a flash of light consumes the viewing frame and the episode ends with screams.

Commentary: When the studio (infrequently) censored *Acres of Perhaps*, it was usually at the scripting stage. In the case of "Ourselves and Immortality," however, one exchange made it to film before being cut, and the clip of objectionable footage is still available on YouTube:

> **Harold**: "I have to be careful who I let in, you know. The future may depend on it."

> **Teresa** (saucily unfolding her legs atop a crate of Army rations): "You can't rebuild a master race by yourself, you know."

Like the rest of the show, "Ourselves" invites a wide range of critical lenses—everything from a historicist look at mid-century nuclear terror to a feminist debate over Teresa's resistance to or complicity with the stultifying patriarchy of the period. It is likely the most commonly taught episode in schools and universities.

Of the episode, Barry Weyrich famously said, "In the toolbox of *Acres of Perhaps*, David was the scalpel and I was the screwdriver. Hugh, poor Hugh, he was the wrecking ball."

The Zodiac Walks on the Moon

Dear Editor:

This is the murderer of the two teenagers last Christmass on Lake Herman Road and the girl a few weeks ago in Vallejo. I phoned a lady dispatcher at the Vallejo Police Department, but she didn't take me seriously. So as not to risk that now, I shall reveal the following details not available to the public:

1. The brand name of the ammunition for the Christmass killing was Super X. I fired ten shots, leaving the boy on his back with his feet to the car and the girl on her right side and her feet to the west.

2. For the more recent killing, the girl was wearing patterned slacks and I used Western ammunition. The boy was shot in the knee.

I hadn't planned to write my first letter until I'd developed the proper voice and taken at least twelve or thirteen victims, but I saw something extraordinary tonight and it has me thinking big things.

A man. Just walked. On the Moon.

I saw it right here on my mother's awful television, as cloudy and grey as her left eye. A little man in a heavy white suit went

47

down a ladder and he said that he was taking a small step for a man but a giant one for mankind. The news people helpfully put LIVE FROM THE MOON on the screen. I think they should have put GODDAM MOON there for good measure.

Like the rest of my neighborhood, I went outside afterward. Some kids down the street set off firecrackers and there's a little boy marching around in long slow strides with a bucket on his head. Their parents are sitting out in lawn chairs with beer bottles heaped at their feet, staring up into space like there's any hope of seeing the glint of that tiny lander.

I understand the impulse to look up, though. To wonder.

I wonder if there will be women on the Moon someday. They'll have to be thin and pretty of course with all of that training, the kind who don't look twice at the wrong men. What will they wear under their suits? Will their boots have heels? Will you see their flowing hair in their helmets or the curves of their breasts under the silver fabric like in all the movies?

I wonder who will be the first to kill one. Will it be the timid geologist who only wanted her soft warmth on his narrow metal bunk? Will it be the strapping Mission Commander whose heroic seed cannot be wasted lest it blast a hole in the LM? Or maybe it will be the man no one ever sees with the wrench in his hand and the grease under his nails.

I wonder how he will do it. There must be lots of ways. He can pull an air hose and let her life hiss away to a sleeping silence. He can drill a hole in the side of her helmet and let the plume of her decompressing blood and brains spray in a graceful arc to the soil. If he doesn't want to fiddle around with that, he could simply shoot her; the bullet would go a lot farther if he missed the first time. Maybe she'd be watching it with awe and disgust when the second one got her in the lady parts. That is where he'd have to aim, with all the junk wrapped around her chest where the heart hides.

And then she'll be there. She'll be there forever, and as the Moon sweeps over our heads, we will know that she's there, that there is a dead woman on the Moon, and the whole thing is nothing more than a giant glowing tombstone.

They'll probably catch the man who does it. Maybe they'll have a trial for him on the Moon, make a little courtroom on the Mare Crisium, the sea of crises. If he's smart, he'll ask for a death by hanging, but they could just as easily put him outside to pound frantically on the reinforced portholes until he totters like a felled tree into the dust.

We will know his name, though, and we will talk forever about why he did it.

I used to think the perfect crime was not getting caught. I was careful with those teenagers and they didn't even see my face, blinded as they were by my lights. I came up on them quickly and they still had their hands deep in each other's pants and skirts, having a ball; I had a ball, too. The ones who ran didn't get far, going down where the bullets told them to. They screamed and thrashed and moaned a little, but no one heard.

The blue meannies will never catch me, and it wasn't even hard. The ammunition is too common and the tire tracks too bald and smeared, and the guns I used are now broken into pieces and spread hither and yon. I didn't know the victims. I live quietly in a distant neighborhood where the little old ladies invite me in for iced tea after I clean their gutters or patch up the front steps.

I used to think the perfect crime was not getting caught, but watching those men tonight changed my mind.

49

In a world where we have landed a flying Volkswagen on the Moon, I think we can expect more from people who die than merely crumpling in a heap, don't you? I think we can expect more from their hunters, too.

I am not going to the Moon. You are not going to the Moon. None of the kids I killed are going to the Moon. But now other people have and we look like a bunch of assholes, missing the toilet with our piss or forgetting to take out the trash, bussing tables at a diner or running numbers in an office.

I will never walk on the Moon. When I am dead, my footprints will be gone.

I used to think the perfect crime was not getting caught and killing as many people as you can, but I'll never reach the heights of Hitler or Stalin, Johnson or Nixon. I'd hoped to be known for the quality of my hunt—the drama and beauty, not to mention my own untouchable safety—instead of the quantity.

But right now, every wakeful eye on Earth is pointed in the same direction, toward the silver island in the dark, and what I'm learning is that an achievement is not an achievement if no one sees it.

The perfect crime is being seen going 240,000 miles farther than anyone else ever has.

This is my Moon. I shall walk in ways men have never walked and kill in ways they have never killed, and I shall tell you all about it so you can tell the world what heights we have finally reached.

I shall strike with such terror that my victoms will only fully know life at the very end, not just teenagers but adults and maybe some kiddies, too. I shall build death machines in an antiseptic room for my mission, flashlight gun sights and remote-trigger bombs, a black hooded spacesuit to recycle the tang of my own breath. I shall write ciphers that only computers can decode. I was going to write beautiful eloquent letters like a gentleman hunter, but now my words will froth on the page in ways that are not exactly mine.

I shall take my name from the eternally watching heavens, but I will not give it to you yet.

This is my Moon landing, and it will take your own room full of men in narrow black ties and horn-rimmed glasses to catch me. I will shift and wobble in parallax with the stars, though, not quite myself when I kill or when I write. And even if you do, it is enough to get to the Moon; coming back can only be disappointing.

This isn't the right letter to send first, I see that now. There is too much of me in it, too much truth, and that's no way to start a mystery. Much better for you to think that I'm insane, barely in control, my letters slashed on the page like knife strokes instead of neatly typed through 3 layers of carbon.

What I shall do instead is fold this neatly into a sealed black metal box and bury it so deep that only the ones who come after us can find it. They will live in the world we make, one that much more vivid and artistic, and they'll want to know who to thank when they send back an expedition from their gleaming bubbled cities in space.

We are now the kind of people who can walk on the Moon, but I am the kind who can kill there. All it takes is one small step.

S1E5: "Singing Each to Each"

Air Date: November 9, 1961
Writer: David Findley
Director: Tim Jokannsen

Synopsis: Recent widower Paul Hansen (played with tragic schlubiness by Norman Westfield) gets up from his desk at a dead-end accounting job and starts to walk with no apparent direction in mind. He wanders through the city, peering forlornly into windows and removing his oppressive suit a little at a time—leaving a hat in the park and his jacket on a fence and his tie in the gutter.

Near sunset, he finds himself at the farthest edge of a jetty. There, after gazing at the sea, he begins to remove his shoes, ready to commit suicide.

Before Paul can leap from the rocks, a beautiful mermaid bobs to the surface nearby. The mermaid (portrayed by Ginger Quinn, tragically dead herself from suicide less than three years later) soothes him with talk of a wondrous world beneath the sea full of hope and beauty and peace. He chooses not to kill himself and returns each day to talk. They clearly fall in love, and on his third visit, she offers to take him away with her. He doesn't hesitate, climbing down the rocks and within her reach. She takes him by the hand and pulls him into the water where she drowns him.

53

As his body floats face down on the surface, she emerges from the water and clearly has two normal human legs instead of a tail. She wraps a towel around herself and walks to shore along the jetty.

Commentary: "Singing Each to Each" marks the first of David Findley's stories to appear onscreen and, not coincidentally, the first to receive a horrified memo from the studio to Hugh Kline. Though the original memo no longer exists, Kline later told fan audiences that the studio objected less to the theme of the episode—which was, after all, a sharp recrimination of dreaming of escape from capitalist society— and more to Quinn's obvious demented glee in her role.

"It wasn't entirely her fault," Kline later explained. "She had this inborn smile that spread about two-thirds of the way around her head like a shark's, and by then she was so high on amphetamines most of the time she probably brushed her teeth like she was choking some poor guy to death."

Six days before her overdose, Ginger Quinn dragged a blood-soaked mattress to the front curb of her Malibu mansion. The source of the blood, a considerable amount, was never publicly disclosed by the LAPD.

The Leaning Lincoln

When I was ten years old, almost all my friends were four inches tall. They drove tanks and piloted spaceships. They rode in my pockets and made camp under napkin tents on restaurant tables. They whispered their emergency plans to me, what we'd do in a fire or a hurricane or a nuclear attack. And at night, they stood on my bookshelves aiming their tiny rifles at the bedroom door, ready for when my father would come thundering in.

He made no secret of hating Star Wars and G.I. Joe—he made no secret of any of the things he hated—and he'd clearly hoped that I'd come from my mother's womb ready to ogle girls and scheme over beers with him. He had no idea why little plastic people were so important to me and I think he woke up almost every morning quietly hoping it would be the day they no longer were, the day when I'd finally grow up and understand as he did that the world was grim and brutal and largely run by assholes.

I did grow up, and I did learn that, and it wasn't my father who taught me but a tiny cursed lead figure of Abraham Lincoln. Unlike my father, though, he taught me what to do about it.

⌘

55

The Leaning Lincoln was a gift from Henry Butler, a man my father met at the gun range.

Henry had been let go as a night janitor at the hospital, and my father's bookstore had been hemorrhaging customers since Christmas to a big box store where the owner didn't tell retirees balking at prices that "it's not the goddamned Depression anymore." Henry helped my dad sight a .22 Remington and my dad spun his usual stories about the coming invasion by the Soviets, and thus a friendship was forged.

When they weren't out shooting watermelons and spray paint cans, they were shooting the shit on our dock by the creek with a heap of beer cans growing between them. That was fine by me; I came to look forward to hearing Henry's tired green Chevy pulling into our gravel driveway.

For one thing, it meant an afternoon when my mother and I weren't going to feel blood pouring down the back of our sinuses after a smack for saying or doing something stupid. For another, Henry loved the things I did but my father hated, like ghost stories and comic books. He had more Atari cartridges than I did and wasn't stingy about trading them. He gave me his old dog-eared fantasy paperbacks, introducing me to Elric and Conan.

Henry could show up at our house with anything from a Confederate cavalry sword to a dinner of Kentucky Fried Chicken, but one afternoon he arrived with a large flat wooden box that seemed to take both hands to carry.

"Hey, look at this, Scotty," my father cried, steering me to the patio table by the shoulders. He had a way of making even something cool seem threatening.

Henry opened the box and started setting up small lead figures, soldiers from the Civil War. There were riflemen

56

marching, cavalrymen with sabers raised, snipers taking aim, cannon loaders with those sticks they use to tamp the gunpowder. There were three or four dozen.

"See, Scotty?" Dad pointed. "You know how I always tell you to keep your eyes open for opportunities?"

Boy, did I. If I didn't come home from a bike ride with a box of nails or some plywood from a construction site, he'd send me out again. He called "scrounging" a valuable post-apocalyptic skill.

He nudged me. "Free lead. You can't beat that, right?"

A few weeks earlier, Henry and my father had taken me clamming in a cove off Palmetto Bay. My job was to fill one bucket with clams while my old man filled another with his empty beer bottles. When we were wading in toward shore at the end of the day, Dad had spied something large and square in the sand. We dug up an ingot of solid lead, about eighteen inches on the long side and a foot on the short. There was a stamped seal on top with words we couldn't make out.

I knew from Indiana Jones where things like that were supposed to go. "It belongs in a museum," I said.

"It's lead, for Christ's sake," Dad muttered, helping Henry load it into the truck. "When opportunity knocks, you don't check its fingernails, you know what I'm sayin'?"

I couldn't imagine how lead could be an opportunity, but Henry could. He liked working with metal, and he annoyed the neighbors from a workshop behind his mother's house at all hours with the sounds of grinding and tapping. He must have found some molds for the soldiers.

"Look at that," my father said, picking up an Abraham Lincoln figure by his fingertips. "The ol' Emancipator himself. Don't remember him doing much fighting."

57

"That one didn't turn out right," Henry said.

My father set the figure on the table and it leaned dangerously forward.

"Kind of looming, isn't he?"

"The legs cooled too fast and contracted," Henry said. Then, brightening, he handed the Lincoln to me. "You want him, Scott?"

I glanced at my father for a sign of his displeasure, but he didn't show any. Maybe it was because the figure was of a real historical thing instead of "that stupid science fiction shit," or maybe it was because it was made of manly lead instead of boyish plastic. More likely, even my old man didn't often dare look like an asshole in front of Henry. Whatever the reason, a cool little guy was a cool little guy, so I took it and thanked Henry.

What a miserable mistake that turned out to be.

⌘

Like Tutankhamen's curse on Carter and Carnarvon, the dread vengeance of that lead ingot came swiftly.

When I put it in my pocket, the small outline of the sixteenth president would always stain through, a tiny exclamation point with a top hat as the dot. When I held it in my hand, it itched and left greasy gray smudges on my skin. When I set it on my dresser or a bookcase, it had a way of tumbling to the floor and finding its way under someone's bare foot, usually mine or my father's.

The Leaning Lincoln's first real victim—an injury, thank God, not a fatality—was Mrs. Catanza's dog Chester, who I hit with my bike while scratching one of those smudges. She'd let him out for his afternoon dump, and I didn't see him galloping towards me down Blackburn Road. Looking up too late, I wobbled to one side, but it was too late to avoid him. The front tire got him in the side and he yelped like he'd been shot.

I screamed, lost my hold on the handlebars, and then tumbled headlong into Mrs. Catanza's rose bushes where it was my turn to yelp. She waddled over to shout at me, taking poor Chester in her arms to soothe while I crawled out of the thorns. All her hollering brought my dad out, cigarette pinched in his lips.

Without saying anything to me or Mrs. Catanza, he picked up my bike, carried it back to the garage, and hung it in the rafters. That was the gentlest way he'd ever grounded me, probably because a neighbor was around.

Over a week, the Leaning Lincoln burrowed a hole in my pocket and burned out the vacuum cleaner motor when it got stuck in the rolling brush. It slowed my watch and made me two hours late for dinner so my mom almost called the cops to find me, earning me a smack from my father after they were gone. It destroyed a load of whites in the dryer with indelible smears of silver. It fell into Bee Gee's water bowl and he whimpered all day with diarrhea until I found it.

It's easy now to see all that as coincidence, but I was a superstitious kid, all confused by cause and effect because in my house, the usual rules between the two didn't apply. What I knew was what I'd read in Henry's copy of *The Lord of the Rings*: certain awful objects could ruin lives and had to be gotten rid of, preferably with a fellowship. So I asked Melanie to help me.

During the school year, Melanie sat behind me in my classes, but I would never have known how cool she was until we started hanging out over the summers. She was also the kind of freak who read books on ghosts and Bigfoot, though I was the kind of freak who took them way more seriously.

Melanie had grown less interested in adventures, but she didn't reject the curse hypothesis when I told her. Her solution was just a little too...simple.

"Throw it away," she said as we walked through the woods between our houses. "Why would you keep it in the first place?"

"We can't do that," I said. "The garbage truck has a long way to go to the dump, and God knows what the Lincoln could do. Roll the truck over? Cut off someone's arm in the compactor?"

"Okay," she said. "Bury it out here, then."

"But then we couldn't use the woods anymore. It'd corrupt the trees or something, leach into the soil."

She turned. "What do you want me to say?"

"I want you to say something useful."

She curled her lip, maybe trying to decide whether to walk off without me or not. She could be touchy that way those days.

Instead, she said, "Well, where did you find it?"

"In the bay, fifty yards offshore in about two feet of water."

"And it was a block?"

"My dad calls it an 'ingot.'"

"Did it have any writing?"

"We saw some kind of stamp but couldn't make it out."

"Ah," Melanie said. "So it's cursed pirate treasure."

See? Once you got her going, she could be cool.

"Lead isn't treasure," I pointed out.

"Sure it is, for pirates. What do you think all those cannonballs were made of? Or the bullets in their guns? Old Gasparilla was on the run in the bay from the Spanish—that's the writing—and he had to drop cargo to escape. Before he did, he cursed it."

Melanie had a way of explaining the ridiculous so that it sounded like reason.

"How does that help us?" I asked.

"It helps a lot," Melanie replied. "It came from the sea, so it has to go back to the sea."

It wouldn't be easy. We were five years too young to drive a car out to Palmetto Bay, and even if we did, the place where we'd found the lead was lined with dense mangroves. My dad had a 10' aluminum SeaKing that could get us out there from our dock, but only he was allowed to use it.

We might not have to go out all that way, though.

"If the water's deep enough, it wouldn't matter where we dropped the Lincoln, would it?"

A few months earlier, I'd seen huge cranes dredging about a hundred feet from the bridge, scooping out silt and mussel shells for some repairs to the pilings. We couldn't throw it that far, but with the help of a hijacked boat...

"I guess it wouldn't," Melanie agreed.

So that was it. We would drop the Leaning Lincoln into the deepest abyss we could find in our little town, just on the other side of the Old Beach Road bridge and within sight of a well-known local seafood restaurant called the Flying Sailfish. We'd borrow my father's boat to get there.

"Great," she said. "Good luck."

"You're coming with me."

She'd been circling the whole Valley Girl thing the last few months, thanks to MTV. She said, "As if. I'm not going to let anybody see me from that restaurant."

"It's a bunch of old people. For all they know, you'd be sunning yourself."

A chance to look glamorous, even to the elderly, wasn't something she could pass up.

⌘

I had to wait until ten in the morning for my father to leave before borrowing his boat. First, he had to finish his morning orange juice with a splash of vodka, then shower and shave, then get dressed, then fiddle around with something on the hot water heater, and then check the oil in the Volkswagen.

Who was running the store those days, I had no idea. Mom had gotten a job as a doctor's office manager so it wasn't her. For all I knew, he opened and closed whenever he felt like it.

When he finally left, I called Melanie to come over. She was wearing shorts over a one-piece bathing suit, plus her mother's huge sun hat. She smeared tanning lotion on her arms while I climbed into the boat in my peeling iron-on *Empire Strikes Back* t-shirt. Then she gingerly extended her right foot before taking the center seat.

If there was any time for turning back, for saving myself another of my father's tooth-loosening punches to the face, this was it. But there was no way I could keep it, and there was no way I could stick someone else with it. The punches were mine to take.

I lowered the 20 horsepower Evinrude so its propeller entered the water. It thunked against the plywood my father had bolted to the back to reinforce it. I pulled out the choke and tugged the rope. I pushed it in about half way and tugged again, but nothing happened. I pushed in the choke and tried again. I put my foot on the gunwale and yanked with all my strength, rocking the SeaKing so hard that it crashed against the sea wall and almost threw us out in the creek.

My old man had adjusted that motor until it was perfect. Now it wouldn't start at all.

Then I remembered the Leaning Lincoln under my seat. I took the coffee can out and gave it to Melanie. She handled it with her towel.

"Put that up in the bow," I said.

The engine then started on the first pull, and I steered us out into the creek. Melanie lounged back in her seat like the lady from *The African Queen*.

Coquina Creek, named for the old Indian mounds along its sides, was wide and shallow near our part, maybe a hundred yards across. We chugged past the little waterfront houses, and the huge tangles of mangrove roots took over from the seawall when we got closer to the bridge. The creek looked wilder there, more adventurous, like an island in a pirate movie.

I idled the motor and we drifted under the Old Beach Road bridge. A couple of cars thump-thumped over as we did, and I nudged one of the pylons so we wouldn't hit it. We passed the deep sandy scars of the cranes, and then the current seemed to pick up.

Above us to my left, the brunch crowd at the Flying Sailfish was lining up for the buffet. A few peered through the windows at us.

"Take the helm," I said to Melanie. She climbed back smiling, brushed the hair from her eyes, and clutched the handle like someone bracing for a typhoon.

I stepped up to the bow, took out the coffee can, and opened the top. I peeled away the paper towels and removed the Leaning Lincoln. In my imagination, it weighed ten pounds and let out a subsonic hum I could feel in my bones.

I held it in my fist above the water.

"Say something," Melanie yelled over the engine noise.

"Okay," I said, taking a breath. "I consign thee to the—"

The boat surged forward with a roar of the Evinrude. I fell back against the gunwale, still clutching the Lincoln. I tottered for a moment, my arms outstretched, and then I fell headfirst into the water.

Even in Florida, even in summer, that water was cold. Or maybe it was the shock that took the air from my lungs. I lost my ability to breathe, not to mention swim, and I felt myself sinking.

Melanie claimed for years afterward that she hadn't turned the throttle. The motor went by itself, she said. If it was late and she was tired, she'd admit it could have been a muscle spasm. If it was later and she was tipsy, she'd say she kind of blacked out for a second and didn't even remember. Like she'd been possessed.

As I let myself sink, the boat zoomed off in a wide arc. I could hear the purr of the engine even under water, something comforting. But then came a muffled squeal and that jarred me into treading water again.

With my eyes barely above the surface, I could see the boat had hit something big. The squeal continued now, and something sharp peeled away an inch-wide tendril of the aluminum hull like a pull top from my father's beer cans. Water gushed in.

I knew what she'd hit. The cranes had dredged a channel in the middle, all right, but they'd piled the razor-sharp mussel shells closer to the restaurant where boats seldom went. Maybe they planned to come get them, or maybe not.

Melanie was shrieking now, which to be fair is what I'd be doing too. I swam over, but the boat was filling up fast. The bow had dipped below the waterline and the stern was swinging over the mussel shells.

My legs scraped against them and the brackish water felt like acid flowing in the cuts. I tried not to scream as I grabbed for Melanie. I was feeling like a real hero, saving the girl with everybody watching.

Then the boat rolled over and knocked me in the head. I dipped below the surface again, and Melanie had to tow me to shore.

God knows what I looked like, blood streaming down my face, to the two dozen white-capped heads watching us from the windows of the Flying Sailfish. Melanie told me later that I held up one hand to say it was all right.

As the boat sank, the motor dragged along the shells, spraying fragments everywhere. It snapped the reinforcing plywood transom, revealing the original name of the boat had been Elizabeth. I gave a limp salute as it went under.

By then, the World War II veterans among the brunch crowd had run down to the shore to throw the decorative life preservers from the restaurant's walls out to us. Melanie grabbed one even though it was made of heavy wood, and we kicked as they pulled us in.

I felt something in my palm and looked down to see I still had the Leaning Lincoln. In all that, I hadn't let go. It hadn't *let* me let go.

Waitresses brought dishtowels to dry us off while the manager called our parents. Everybody knew I was the bookstore owner's son so there was no hope of them calling Mom instead. All I could do was wait for him to come.

Melanie's mother pulled up in their Datsun first and willed her daughter inside with a terrifying glare.

I waved to say, "See you later!" but neither waved back.

Eventually, a sputtering Volkswagen on the road above signaled my reckoning. I stepped away from the other people in case my father decided to run me over.

He didn't. He stopped, climbed out, and peered at me. In certain moments, among certain watching eyes, my father could be eerily calm and focused. A man who would give you a smack across the chops for not blowing your nose could gaze contemplatively at his drenched and bloody son.

"You okay?" he said.

"Yeah," I replied. "The boat—"

He opened the passenger door and waited for me to climb inside. He then approached a waitress with his wallet open.

"How much do I owe you for those towels?"

She shook her head and he leaned in for a smarmy wink.

Before he could climb into the car himself, though, a man came up and tapped him on the shoulder.

"Sir?" my father said.

"Where'd you get a boat like that oldie?"

"Want ads," he replied, getting into the seat.

"You sure?" the man asked.

My father put the key in the ignition. "Yeah."

"Because, heh," the man said, rubbing the back of his own neck, "I'm missing a boat just like it. Lost her a few months ago when I was out of town. Named her Elizabeth. Thought the storm broke her free from the dock."

66

I could imagine the boat drifting, drifting, thumping against our own dock with a broken rope. I could also imagine my father not checking the fingernails of an opportunity.

"Huh," my father said, snapping the Beetle into reverse. "Sorry I can't help you, buddy."

⌘

My concussion saved me a beating from my father; the last thing he needed was a second set of hospital bills. Mostly he yelled. About responsibility. About sneaking around. About the sanctity of people's property.

I was grounded of course, not that I felt much like going outside with my head hurting like it did. My books and figures got taken away, too, all but the Leaning Lincoln. I was supposed to sit in my room and contemplate my sins, I guess.

My dad had a lot to contemplate, too. A few days after the voyage, a letter arrived via certified mail from the man who'd owned the boat: he was a lawyer, naturally, asking politely for my father to pay for it. My father knew those letters always started politely but never ended that way.

Dad was the kind of man who borrowed a Cadillac to drive to Rotary meetings, who'd overextended to buy a small house to say it was "on the water." He didn't care as much about losing money as he did about losing its appearance.

"Having a million dollars isn't success," he used to say. "Being trusted to borrow a million dollars is."

If he'd ever had that trust, he'd lost it now. Bad enough the town banker knew he'd missed loan payments. Bad enough the lady at the electric company knew he'd charmed her into letting the bill slide a month or two. But to be a thief was too much.

Though no one closed the door to him at the Rotary, fewer came to shake his hand. And that was worse.

Mom worked later and later, and though she wanted me to rejoin the Boy Scouts or play some sport, my father insisted I stay with him. Mostly, we would work on one of his crazy projects—trying to splice the neighbor's cable, running pipes for a well—and then he'd make me cook a "frontier" dinner of mushy spaghetti or burnt hamburgers. We'd eat in lawn chairs while he held forth. Big corporations were pushing out the little guys. There were too many spinner racks of paperbacks in the grocery store. The Good Ol' Boys in Florida wouldn't buy from a New Yorker. The loan officer wanted to sleep with Mom.

One of those nights, my dad was flying—it had been a bad day thanks to a foreclosure notice served in front of customers. We were eating quietly from camping bowls when Henry arrived. I was relieved to see him lumbering across our yard toward the dock, but the closer he got, the more frightened I became.

His eyes had sunken even more into his skull and the shadows around them had gone gray—the gray of lead, I imagined. His hair, usually slick and black against his head, had lost its color; he'd aged twenty years in weeks. Even his clumsy and irregular gait was now close to a stagger.

68

"Jesus, Henry," my father said, turning around. "What the fuck happened to you?"

Henry stood a moment in our yard, staring over our heads at the setting sun. Water clopped against the seawall and he closed his eyes as though to listen.

"Sit down, for Christ's sake," my old man said, motioning me out of my chair.

I was happy to oblige, and I even reached to help. Henry smiled weakly at me and let me guide him to the chair.

"You sick or something?"

I saw Henry's fingers curl around the aluminum armrest. They were smudged, not like my father's with nicotine but gray. His sweat even smelled metallic. He seemed to creak and I wasn't sure if it was his joints or the chair's.

I leaned in to tell him to get rid of the lead, that it was cursed or poisonous or radioactive or something, but he spoke before I could.

"I've felt better," Henry said.

My father peeled open an Old Milwaukee for him. Henry lifted it for a sip. After he'd swallowed, he reached into the front pocket of his jumpsuit and gave my father a folded yellow piece of paper.

My father opened it and held it far from his face because he'd refused to believe his eyesight was failing.

"You got evicted?" he squeaked. "From your own fucking house? How does that happen?"

"It's not my house," Henry said, simply. "It never was, according to Ben's lawyer." Ben was his brother, the one fighting him for their mother's estate. "I've been squatting, they say."

Good, I thought. Now he'll get away from that shed and all the lead inside.

"That's bullshit. Come stay with us."

Henry shook his head. "I've got a line on a night auditor job at the Motel 8. They might let me take a room for a few weeks."

"What did Matthews say?"

Matthews was Henry's lawyer.

69

"He said there isn't much to do until the mediation. That could be months. Nobody but me is in a hurry."

Neither noticed I was pretending to read *Chariots of the Gods* by the dying light. Books have a way of making you invisible.

"I don't know why I even want that house," Henry said. "I don't belong here."

"In Florida?" My dad took a gulp of beer. "You and me both, pal. Nothing but old farts and rednecks living on a sandbar."

"No," Henry said slowly. "I mean, I don't belong anywhere. Not now, anyway."

For someone who owned a bookstore, my old man wasn't exactly glowing with imagination. To him, you were where you were and there wasn't anything to do about it. But I understood what Henry was talking about: I'd too felt disappointed that books and life were so different and wondered which was wrong. Sometimes I still do.

"There's nothing for me here," he said. "There's too much getting along."

"Amen, brother." My father crinkled the empty can in his fist and dropped it to the deck with a thunk. "Civilization is overrated, as folks will discover when the Russians come knocking."

Maybe he did have an imagination.

My dad then clapped Henry on the back. "Let me show you something I got. It'll cheer you up."

Henry didn't look like he wanted cheering up, but my dad went inside and came out again holding a rifle against his side like that picture of Lee Harvey Oswald.

He fiddled with it dramatically as he always did, slapping in an empty magazine, cocking it, dry firing it. I ducked away each time the barrel swung in my direction. This was a man, after all, who'd once put a .38 bullet into our dining room table while I was sitting at it.

"Chinese surplus Norinco SKS," he said, holding it out. "All she needs is a guy good with metal to get 'er full auto."

Henry took it from him wordlessly. He checked the chamber and removed the magazine before squinting down the sights at a clump of mangrove in the creek.

"I can do that," said Henry.

My father sighed. "Too bad a bunch of psychos keep guys like us from having the tools we need."

Henry didn't reply.

"Guns are wasted on those nutjobs shooting up a post office or a fucking McDonalds when there's a whole world of assholes who really need it."

"Yeah," Henry said.

"Like that crooked lawyer. Whose side is he on? You'd sure find out with a barrel pointing in his face."

Henry scared me then, staring out at the water, not saying something reasonable. A chunk of driftwood had caught on the dock pilings and made a soft slurping sound.

"And that fucking banker taking my store." Dad took the SKS and aimed it out across the creek. "Pop, pop, pop!"

Henry didn't say anything.

"You don't have to get all the assholes. God knows there aren't enough bullets in the world. But get a few and scare the rest, right?"

"You'd end up in jail, though," Henry said. "You wouldn't be able to take care of your family."

"That's why guys like us don't do it. You've got to get someone who doesn't give a shit anymore, maybe dying or

71

whatever. He takes one for the team, pooling up everybody's enemies and shooting them in one afternoon. He'd be a hero."

Oh, no, Dad. Shut up. Shut up.

"Who would you add to the list?"

"Theoretically?" My father didn't take long to think about it. He flipped out his fingers one by one to count them off. "Your shyster Matthews, of course. Weiss the banker, too. That bitch who keeps trying to kick my bookstore out of the shopping center. That old Nazi down the block here who probably poisoned our cat sniffing around his garden. That blowhard at the Better Business Bureau, what's-his-name with the bow tie."

Henry nodded.

"Funny how five bullets could solve all our problems," Dad said.

I thought of the Leaning Lincoln, encased in another coffee can on my closet's top shelf. I thought, too, about the many bullets the rest of the lead could make.

Dad looked down at the rifle. "That's what I keep these for. Like people who buy lottery tickets to imagine what they'd do if they won. I imagine what I'd do if nothing mattered anymore."

My father talked and talked, and Henry listened. They drank far into the night, my father way more than Henry, and when it was time to go home, Henry took the rifle with him.

⌘

One cloudy afternoon a week later, I rode my bike home from the library and saw Henry's truck wasn't in the driveway like usual. I slowed my pace to postpone getting home, but it couldn't last forever. I eventually had to go inside, opening the door as silently as I could.

"What are you sneaking around for?" demanded my father's voice from the kitchen.

I froze. "Nothing."

"You afraid of me?" he said, stepping into the archway. He filled it, tall and wide as he was. He had a short glass of heavily diluted orange juice.

Uh, oh. I had no idea what the right response would be. Did he want me to be afraid? Did he not? Either way, I had to hurry with an answer because the pause would be worse.

"No," I said.

"They're saying things about me, your little friends, the sons and daughters of the town worthies? About the thief?"

When I was within reach, he grabbed me by the back of the neck. He pulled me closer, pinching. Soon my face was so close to his that I could smell orange juice, vodka, cigarettes. My father, in other words.

I tried to tell him no, but he shook me hard enough to see stars. I closed my eyes to keep them in my skull. If only Henry could come. If only he'd been a little late, a little distracted, still on his way.

The next best thing happened. The phone rang.

It was my old man's turn to freeze. He'd stopped answering the phone because of bill collectors, but it kept ringing long after they'd have given up.

His fingers released my neck and he grabbed the olive-green receiver hanging on the wall. "Hello?"

There was a long silence.

"Henry?" he said, letting out a laugh. "What the hell are you doing there? You get pulled over?"

73

My father's smile faded. His eyes changed like they sometimes did toward the end of beating my mother or me, when he'd recovered enough conscience to wonder how he'd ever make good again. Then they tightened again, confident.

"Well, don't tell them anything," he said. "There's nothing to tell. You want me to start calling around for a real lawyer?" He rubbed his hand across his stubbled crew cut while Henry answered. "Okay, if you've got it, that's fine." He listened again. "Well, take care of yourself, buddy."

By then, Mom had come home from work. She wore her comfortable white shoes with the thick soles, but she still sighed when she sat down at the kitchen table. She was untying one before she noticed my father and I were silent.

"What happened?" she asked.

My father probed the inside of his mouth with his tongue in thought. Then, he reached into the refrigerator for a beer.

"Henry's in the Sarasota County jail," he said. He cracked open the beer and watched it foam through the tiny hole. He shook his head and chuckled. "That screwball killed Matthews."

"What?" Mom sat up. "Why would he do that? What happened?"

"How the hell should I know?" my father snapped. "The guy was always a little weird, wasn't he?"

It was true the only adult I'd ever seen playing with metal army men was Henry, and he'd made the crack-crack noises of guns going off when he did. I'd thought that was a good thing, myself; it made me think I didn't have to grow up to be like my father. But under the influence of that lead, he'd become something else.

"What if it wasn't his fault?" I asked, quietly.

74

My father scowled at me like I was crazy. "They found him with the rifle, Scotty." As though that closed the case.

⌘

Mom cut out all the articles from the *Osprey Herald*.

On the afternoon of the murder, Mr. Matthews and two of his associates had gone to the Osprey Golf and Country Club to play a few rounds. Somewhere around the seventh hole near a stand of scrub pines, they saw a man lurking in the woods wearing an olive drab mechanic's suit and carrying a golf bag. The golf bag was horizontal, though, and they didn't see any clubs in it.

They said the man came shuffling out of the trees toward them, almost as though injured. They'd wanted to laugh, said one, because the guy looked so out of place. Mr. Matthews craned his neck to see who it was, and when he saw, he grabbed at his associate's shirt sleeve.

By then, Henry was reaching in the bag for my father's SKS, now converted to full auto. He slid it out by the barrel, pulling a few inches at a time before he got it free. Then he swung it around to spray the men and their golf cart. One of them got hit in the knee and rolled out of sight. The other ran across the fairway. Mr. Matthews tumbled back across the golf cart, his hands raised.

According to the man now hiding nearby, Henry didn't say anything. He replaced the magazine, aimed the rifle at Matthews's chest, and burned through another clip. What was left of Mr. Matthews slid from the other side of the cart.

Henry gazed out across the fairway into the cloudy glare. He dropped the rifle next to the cart and reached into the bag again. This time, he pulled out his .22 Explorer pistol and walked toward where the witness was lying.

The man slumped deeper against the grass, hoping he'd look dead. Henry stood above him a moment, holding the pistol over the man's head with a swaying circular motion. Then, doing nothing, he limped back toward the woods.

"Jesus," my mother said when she read that.

Henry climbed into his truck, hidden on an access road. He backed up in a spray of gravel and drove off.

According to authorities, he went next to a Circle K store where he bought a Dr. Pepper. He drank it inside, coaching a kid playing the Gyruss machine. Then he went back out to his truck and peeled back a tarp to fiddle with something before taking off again.

By now, the local sheriff's deputies were searching along the two major highways into and out of town, but Henry wasn't leaving. He headed toward the business district. There, seen by security cameras, he circled the Osprey Bank and Trust six times before parking in a handicapped spot near the entrance. He sat a few minutes, a darkened shadow in the cab barely visible to the camera.

As Henry's bad luck would have it, an off-duty police officer had been depositing his paycheck in the drive-thru when he heard on his radio that a green Chevy pick-up had been implicated in a murder. He saw it parked in front of the bank and called for backup.

Henry was climbing out when a Sarasota County police cruiser thumped its wheels over the curb and nearly t-boned the truck and Henry with it. Henry pulled his twin .357 Colt revolvers with his hand-carved grips from his belt and raised them. The deputy in the car ducked behind his door, but by

76

then the off-duty cop had tackled Henry from behind. One of the revolvers went off and shattered a bank door.

In Henry's truck under the tarp, they found three other guns and twenty-five hundred rounds. In his left front pocket, they found a list of names.

⌘

It took a few weeks for Henry's public defender to come talk to my father. He sure wasn't hard to find those days; the store had closed for good and my father spent his afternoons burning files in the fire circle he'd built in our backyard. I can only imagine what the lawyer thought walking up to this sunburned man wearing swim trunks feeding invoices to the flames on a ninety-degree day.

I don't know if he saw me or not, sitting on one of the higher branches of our tree reading Sherlock Holmes stories. I did a lot of lurking after the murder, maybe because I didn't know what else to do. The quieter I was, the harder it was for my father to find me.

The defender held his free hand up to his eyes as a shade; the other held a briefcase.

"Mr. Wrenwood?"

My father looked up. "What can I do for you?"

"I'm James Milona, Henry Butler's defense attorney."

"Huh. How's that going?" he asked.

Milona shrugged. "Could be better," he admitted. "Lots of gaps to fill, questions to answer."

"Yeah, I'm sure."

Milona nodded at the burning papers. "Taking care of some business?"

My old man could muster an expression of innocence faster than anybody. "Oh, this?" he asked, as though he'd stumbled on it. "I'm disposing of old documents. The store's closed, don't need them anymore. Lawyers do that, too, don't they?"

Milona conceded they did. He waited a moment, staring at the flames. Then he asked, "What do you think happened?"

"To Henry?" My father shrugged. "I wish I knew. He seemed pretty level-headed most of the time, but I guess that's what they always say about killers."

Killers. He'd called Henry a killer.

"Was Mr. Butler a violent man, do you think?"

My father tore out a few more invoices and let them slide into the fire. "I guess anybody is, if you push him enough."

"Had Mr. Butler said anything? Made any threats? Seemed...different?"

"He was always different, never quite right in the head, a little 'touched' as you Southerners call it."

I crushed my paperback above them in the tree, angry that he was throwing his friend to the fire as surely as he was those papers. I wanted to yell, "Bullshit!" but I knew it wouldn't help.

Milona nodded. "You might be right. He doesn't say much, even to me. He knows they've got him and his only hope is to give us some mitigating factor—depression, passion, rage—to keep him from the electric chair, but he isn't talking."

"Probably a good idea," my father grumbled.

"Won't look good to a jury, though. Neither will the bullets."

"How's that?"

"He made them himself. It looks a little creepy, like premeditation, when you reload old 7.62mm brass from the range with bullets you cast yourself. Looks a little meticulous. They shredded after impact."

"Huh," my dad said.

"Then there's the list he had, those other victims he didn't even know."

My father was wily enough to pause before asking, "Oh? What other victims?"

"Five names but he was connected directly to one. The others are bankers, business people, a shopping center manager—random, almost."

My old man spoke slowly now. "Well, he was a weird guy. Maybe he thought he was doing us all a favor, starting with the people everybody loves to hate."

"Maybe so." Milona reached into his briefcase and pulled out a card. "Why don't you take this in case anything comes to you? He's going to need all the help he can get, and if you think of anything...you know."

"Right."

"We might even need you to testify," Milona said. "Character witness, that kind of thing."

The irony of my father being anybody's character witness would have made me slip from the tree if I wasn't clenching the branch.

"Well, you take care, Mr. Wrenwood. We'll all do our best for Henry."

My father waited until the defender was halfway across the lawn with his back turned before dropping the card into the fire, too.

⌘

I stopped sleeping after that, at least the whole night through. My father wasn't sleeping either, though we both stayed on our own sides of the house—him at the kitchen table smoking in the darkness, me reading under the blankets with a flashlight.

Henry wouldn't say anything, I knew. He had one other thing in common with a kid, in common with me: he'd read too many books about being a hero to give someone else up in his place.

I could tell them what I knew. I could find Mr. Milona's name in the phone book and call him and explain that I'd heard my father listing all those names. I could tell him the SKS was his, too, purchased from a friend-of-a-friend without any registration.

Then in the hours or days it took to arrest him, my father could kill me. Worse, he could kill my mother. He could barricade himself in the house to make one last stand before the world.

I could tell Mom what I knew, though by the time the school year was ready to start, she had taken a second job at night as an EMT and was hard to catch alone. She'd come home exhausted wearing her blue county uniform with the white doctor's office one on a hanger, ready to swap them again after six hours of sleep.

80

I caught her as she woke up one morning and helped her unfold her glasses from the nightstand.

"Scotty," she said. "Are you okay?"

It was like everything I wanted to say got jammed in my throat before reaching my mouth. I swallowed, but nothing would come out.

She sat up and pulled me close, which is something I hadn't known I needed.

"It's not always going to be like this," she told me. "I promise."

"What?"

"Your life. You're going to go away to college someday, have a family, become a good man."

That seemed impossible. I hadn't thought much about what I'd do for a living because, well, I never figured I'd grow up.

"What about you, Mom?"

She smiled sadly. "I'm not going anywhere."

I'd held it in until then, but that's when I cried. I couldn't say it, but I'd have given up being born if it would have kept her away from my father.

"Not without you," she said into my hair.

I didn't mention Henry. Sitting there with Mom, skulking at the edges of my father's hurricane hoping not to get swept out to sea, it was a lot harder. He'd taught us for years that he was the power of our lives, and he would always win.

⌘

Normal kids have projects, but I always had schemes: weird, labyrinthine plans with big theoretical payoffs and ten times the usual effort. I guess the apple doesn't fall far from the tree as they say. I'm surprised it took me as long as the start of the school year to think of one to stop my father, but by then, the aura of that Leaning Lincoln had probably seeped into all our brains.

A scheme required a fellow schemer, and though she'd been avoiding me ever since the fiasco at the Flying Sailfish, Melanie had to have cooled off by then, right?

81

We had a signal for when we wanted to meet at our old fort in the woods: one of us would set a pine cone in the window of the other. But when the window didn't work that fall, I started putting them by her front door, the back door, on the hood of her mother's car.

I waited every day for her after school in the woods, and I was almost ready to go home when she stepped through the curtain of pine needles from the real world and into the one that had once been ours. Just inside, she stood with her arms folded.

"I'm here to tell you to knock it off. The pine cone crap, I mean."

"Where have you been?" I asked.

"Same places I always am," she replied.

"Are you okay?" I looked her over for visible injuries. "After the boat and all—"

"I'm fine," she said. "See?"

She lifted her leg beside me, long and soft-looking. On the underside, though, was a crooked pink furrow where she'd been scraped by the mussel shells.

"Jeez, I'm sorry," I said. "I didn't—"

"Did you want to talk about something?"

She wasn't going to sit down, and I might not have much time.

82

"Did you hear about Henry?"

"Did I hear about Henry? You mean the psychotic who shot his attorney with a machine gun at my father's country club? No, they've kept that pretty quiet around here."

"He didn't do it because he was crazy."

She closed her eyes. "If you say he did it because of the lead, I swear I'll never talk to you again. For real."

Well, the lead was involved, but that wasn't what I meant.

"He did it because my father told him to."

She didn't say anything but her eyes locked onto mine.

"They were drinking and my father had all these ideas, and Henry always wants to do things for us like we're his family, and I think he thought he was saving us."

"You think this or you know it?"

"I heard them."

She sat down then on a milk crate. "Who are you going to tell?"

I could have rattled off the candidates, but I'd already dismissed them.

"You have to, you know."

Once, when my mother had gathered the courage to tell my father she was going to leave him, he shoved her into the corner of the kitchen and swore he'd kill us all and then himself if she did. He wouldn't let his own son send him to prison without a fight.

"We couldn't get away fast enough. He'd get out on bail and then it'd be all over."

I didn't have to convince Melanie. She'd seen the bruises and had an instinctive revulsion to my old man of her own—somehow resistant to his requests to "come over with your bathing suit and go swimming in the creek."

"You have to do it anyway," she said quietly. Then, because she always knew where to hit me, she added, "That's what they do in books, isn't it?"

It was what they did in books, yes, but people in books had more inside them than I ever would.

"He'd hurt my mom."

83

"You've got to tell her to get away, then." She moved her head closer into my sight so I'd look at her. Her hair smelled of lemon and the long blonde strands hid one side of her face.

I didn't say anything.

"Scott, this is someone's life."

"I know. It's a bunch of people's lives. But I think I can save them all if you hear me out."

She drifted away now.

"No, I've got a plan. Here it is: we use the lead against my father. We get all of it we can, all those soldiers from Henry's shop, and we surround the guy. We let the radioactive waves or whatever get into his head so he goes ape-shit on the witness stand." It made perfect sense, saying it aloud.

Melanie frowned and it was the worst thing I'd ever seen. I'd have taken fifty punches to the face from my old man not to have that expression aimed at me. It seemed so final.

I knew I'd lost her. She was one step ahead or behind me, whichever, but we were out of sync, possibly forever. She didn't believe anymore.

She stood up. "You can't wait for magic to do the things you're supposed to do."

Then she stepped back through the pines and was gone.

I ended up hiding the Lincoln in my father's pillow, but if it gave him as much as a bad dream, he never showed it.

⌘

In February, my father was called to testify on the third day of Henry's trial. He whistled in the mirror that morning, adjusting the tie of the same silver-gray business suit he'd worn while applying for the small business loan at Osprey Bank and Trust.

"No, sir," he said to his reflection. "I loaned him the rifle as one hobbyist to another. I thought he'd take out his frustration on the range. I never expected tragedy."

Jesus, I thought. Was the Lincoln helping him?

"Yes, sir. He seemed a gentle man. Kept to himself. Generous with my son. That's him sitting over there. He could tell you what a good man Henry usually was."

Yeah, I would be sitting there. My old man had taken me out of school for the day, probably so there'd be at least two people afraid of him in the courtroom, me and my mom.

"I thank God that law enforcement stopped him," my father said.

Mom and I looked at each other, not saying anything. She was tired, I could see, tired of his bullshit in the mirror.

As my parents drank the last of their coffee in the kitchen, I unzipped the pillow and took out the Leaning Lincoln. I had a feeling he could come in handy.

Dad drove us to Sarasota, waving people in when they needed to merge, smiling at the waitress at IHOP, tipping her with a twenty. He was confident as we climbed the steps to the courthouse, too, his suit jacket open like a lost Kennedy brother boarding a Lear jet.

Then he saw the metal detector.

About two weeks before Henry's trial, an angry grandfather pulled a gun at a child support hearing in Pensacola and fired it over the judge's left shoulder before being tackled by bailiffs. These were the days before metal detectors were common in government buildings, but they sure started popping up afterward. Sarasota County was one of the first.

My old man stopped at the security station, not letting his smile slip. I wonder if he thought it was for him. I hoped so.

85

He walked up. A deputy held out a plastic bucket. My father unclasped his watch and dropped it inside. Then he emptied his change. Without asking, he stepped through the detector.

It beeped.

Laughing, my father backed up patting his pockets again.

"Your belt, sir," the deputy said.

"Ah." My dad unclasped it, rolled it up, and put it in the bucket, too. "If you wanted me to take off my pants, you just had to ask," he said, winking to a woman behind us in a suit. She turned out to be Henry's prosecutor.

My father leaned to go through again and with an agility I'd learned from years of magic kits, I slipped the Leaning Lincoln into the pocket of his jacket. It was my last hope. All they'd have to do was analyze it, find out it was the same lead...

The detector cried out again. This time, my father wasn't smiling as he stepped back. He patted his jacket this time, felt the hard metallic lump, and reached inside.

The Lincoln looked smaller in his hand than it ever had in mine. He stared down at it and then turned to me. His lips grew taut against his teeth. He leaned over a trash can and dropped Lincoln inside. It echoed like a shot against the metal.

If I'd known it was that easy, I would have given it to him months earlier.

This time, the detector let him through. It let Mom and me through, too. I glanced into the can down at the Leaning Lincoln. Whatever curse he'd borne, my father was worse.

⌘

The trial went badly for Henry from the start. In the days before my father's testimony, the prosecutor he'd annoyed at the metal detector called eleven eyewitnesses, plus experts who'd matched the firing pin and ejector of the SKS to marks on spent casings on the scene. A metallurgist compared the unusual low-quality lead of the bullets with samples from Henry's workshop. The two deputies who'd nabbed him told their stories with a self-satisfied machismo better suited to men who'd bagged John Dillinger than two small-town cops catching a tired old man by accident.

Milona cross-examined as best he could.

Henry sat at the defense table with his hands folded in his lap. Unlike guys in the movies keeping up their poker faces, he looked horrified and ashamed as though he was surprised to be there.

Mom, Dad, and I sat two rows from the front on one of those hard wooden courtroom pews. Mom clutched her purse, flexing and releasing and then flexing again. My old man leaned forward with one elbow on his knee like someone watching a close basketball game.

Milona called my father to the stand after lunch. He stepped up the aisle smiling and buttoning his jacket. He took the oath, and the Bible didn't burst into flames as I'd hoped and half-expected.

This was it. If there was one thing a courtroom was good for, it was making guilty men squirm, at least on TV. I waited for my dad to crack, for the Leaning Lincoln to have weakened his will, but oh, no.

He answered every question with charm, saying the lines he'd practiced and winging the others. He paused and stammered enough to seem shocked to be there, but not so much that he seemed scared.

There'd been some question about Henry's "obsession" with firearms, so Milona asked, "Mr. Wrenwood, are you and Mr. Butler 'gun nuts'?"

My father glanced at the jury. "No, sir, I wouldn't say that. A gun is a tool. Being a nut for one would be like being a hammer nut or a wrench nut."

That got a chuckle out of the crowd, the judge included. I watched them all amazed. Why couldn't they see?

Milona kept him on the stand longer than the other witnesses he called. The questions went deeper, too, circling the exact origin of Henry's idea to shoot his lawyer and four strangers.

"Did he ever talk about murder?" Milona asked.

"Not in any specific sense, no."

"What sense, then?"

"You know," my father said. "The sense of a tired and angry man feeling cornered late in his life. I thought he was blowing off steam, but..."

Milona put his fingers to his brow, considering the next question. He knew, I could tell. Or he suspected. But if he was hoping to crack my old man, he'd need a good one.

"Did *you* ever talk about murder, Mr. Wrenwood?"

Oh, no. That wasn't it. How could he not know you couldn't fight him head-on? Even Lincoln couldn't.

My father knew this was a time for earnestness more than charm, so his expression went grave.

"No," he said. "I never have. And I'll tell you why. I'm too selfish to kill anybody. I've got too much to live for, a wonderful wife and son. I've had setbacks like Henry, and I worry he decided to solve them for me from some sense of, I don't know, heroism or something."

It was like a speech from a movie. I'm sure he'd practiced it until it sounded perfect. Some of the jury members nodded.

"I wish he hadn't," he concluded.

Milona closed his eyes. "No more questions," he said. It was over.

My father descended from the stand, smiled humbly at the jury, and returned to our pew.

It couldn't be over.

He took Mom's shaking hand and patted it. He squeezed my knee like he held the gearshift of the Volkswagen.

It was all over.

There were other witnesses and a sidebar on some issue of the law, but I didn't notice. My body couldn't decide between crying and throwing up so it just clenched inward. I was hot and then cold and then hot again.

The Leaning Lincoln hadn't worked. No matter how hard I'd tried to find it, magic didn't come through. Which was what Melanie had been trying to tell me.

What sucked the most to me then was the thought that my father had been right: no matter how safe they'd made me feel, those action figures really were nothing but plastic, the movies they were in nothing but film, the books nothing but paper. Whatever I'd thought was a curse was just what it was like to grow up, trading plastic for lead.

The Leaning Lincoln wasn't bad luck. The Leaning Lincoln was life.

I heard the crack of the wooden hammer but only vaguely perceived people getting up for a recess.

"Thank God," my father muttered. "I've had to piss like a race horse for the last half an hour."

89

If there was any magic at all in the world, something would have struck him down right then. It was a terrible thing to pray for, but I did.

"Come on," I whispered. "You're going to let him go?"

I wondered who the 'you' was. God? The Universe? Anyone else but me?

Standing now, I watched my father's square shoulders disappear through the courtroom doors with the other people. None of them knew. They didn't feel it coming off him.

I felt Mom's touch on my arm.

"I'm ready if you are," she said, simply.

I wasn't sure what she meant at first. I must have looked at her like she was crazy.

"To go," she said.

That's when I got the first inkling that Mom hadn't been leaving me behind on all those nights. She was finding a way out. She nodded, watching me realize what she was saying.

So magic or not, I slipped between the adults standing in the aisle, ducked under their arms and dodged their steps, and I pushed open the little oak gate beside the defense table.

Henry heard me first and turned. He smiled when he saw me—at his own trial, can you believe that? I smiled back. He opened his mouth to say something but I forced myself away, forced myself to tap Milona on the shoulder.

"Sir?" I said.

The attorney turned. Seated, he was at my eye level. "What can I do for you?"

"I know something," I said. "I heard something."

He considered, looking not at all surprised. "Does your mother know you're talking to me?"

I looked back. She was sitting straight in the courtroom pew, watching us. Milona tilted his head toward the stand with an unspoken question. She closed her eyes and nodded.

When the gavel fell again and the court was back in session, Milona asked to approach the bench.

⌘

So I was the action figure. I testified and saved Henry from the electric chair but not life in prison. That life was short—he died eight years into his sentence—and I never spoke or wrote to him because there was nothing to say. Sorry my father was evil? Thanks for saving us from him as long as you did?

During the rest of Henry's trial, Milona put us up in a hotel a few towns over, expensed to protect us as witnesses but also to buy us time. He persuaded the prosecutor to have my father picked up on conspiracy, solicitation, firearms charges, anything that would stick even briefly. We had four hours before he made his bail to carry out our suitcases. Mine had the Millenium Falcon jammed inside with my clothes.

But the cops investigated and they kept an eye on him, making him act human long enough for Mom to make the arrangements with the money she'd been hiding to get us back up north and living with my grandparents. It was hard on only her income, and there wasn't much magic in those years except what we got from frozen dinners together in front of the television. Quiet. Together. Safe.

My dream was for my father to go to prison, for my mother to testify about everything he did and was, for me to tell that courtroom that he was the one worse even than Henry. It turns out, though, that suggesting a murder isn't quite a crime.

Neither—quite—is loaning a rifle to a man who happens to use it for one. My father hid his whole life behind "quite."

And for the rest of that life, I was his amateur parole officer. We didn't speak, we didn't exchange letters or cards—I only checked for his name in the Florida legal databases. He remarried and his new wife died. He remarried again and she died, too. He had a few brushes with the law, including an investigation into the third wife's car accident, but nothing stuck. If the Leaning Lincoln had affected him at all, I couldn't tell the difference from his sad declining life.

I did see him at the end. The hospice called me, having looked up my name online. They told me the cancer had spread from the colon, a cancer I hadn't known or cared about, and if I wanted to see my father, it had to be soon.

Lindsey tried to talk me out of going and it almost wasn't hard, but in the end, I just wanted to know what he'd say.

I found him in his bed beside a large window facing the woods. His head was all I could see above the sheets and the body beneath them seemed withered to a stalk. I'm sure if I got him to his feet, he'd lean like that Lincoln until he fell.

His sunken eyes locked onto me, and I'll admit I allowed myself an instant of hope that I'd see something in them that had grown or blunted or tamed with thirty years. I didn't. They hardened quickly and the thin lips drew tautly into a rueful smile as though to ask what I was hoping to see. What I was hoping to get.

"Hey, Dad," I said, sitting down beside the bed. I don't know if he could talk or not, but he didn't. "I brought you something."

I set the Leaning Lincoln I'd recovered from that courthouse trash can on the cheap plastic table holding the cups with their straws for his liquid nutrition. My father glanced at the lead figurine with annoyance and then back at me with more.

I wanted to tell him that the Lincoln had been harmless to me and Lindsey and the kids, but he didn't deserve to know that. I wanted to tell him that there were still little toy people in my home long after he had gone, that there'd always been books and movies and fantasy in our lives, but he didn't deserve to know that, either. So I didn't say anything, just kept sitting beside that bed and watching the Lincoln work on my father and my father work on Lincoln, wondering who would win.

In two hours, the Lincoln did.

S1E10: "Guess What's Coming to Dinner?"

Air Date: December 14, 1961
Writer: Barry Weyrich
Director: Dean "Deano" McDonald

Synopsis: Shirley McDougall (Francine Thomasin) and her daughter Penny (Judith Affelt) are preparing dinner while little brother Ralph (Timmy Harwood) sets the table and father Bruce McDougall (Cabe Phillips in the first of his ubiquitous appearances) nervously adjusts his tie in a mirror.

The doorbell rings and Shirley opens it. Standing on the doorstep is a seven-foot tall lizard man in a perfect business suit. He smiles as best he can and holds out a bottle of sludge-like wine which Shirley graciously accepts. Mr. McDougall shakes hands with the visitor (whose name seems to be Mr. Grggit) and motions him to the dinner table where an awkward meal ensues. Mrs. McDougall serves a casserole dish of writhing grubs that Mr. Grggit eats, regurgitates, and then re-eats while everyone gazes down at their own plates. Politics comes up and everyone agrees with Mr. Grggit's pronouncements about hard work. Religion comes up and everyone agrees that the Sky Bird is kind and generous.

After the meal is over, Ralph performs a song and Mr. Grggit claps his claws in approval. Mr. Grggit then thanks everyone for the wonderful meal, shakes Mr. McDougall's hand, and tucks Ralph under his arm. Ralph cries and reaches for his

95

mother, but Mrs. McDougall can only look helplessly on as he takes him away.

After they leave, she holds her husband close and says, "Do you think you'll keep the job?" and Mr. McDougall replies, "I hope so, dear. I hope so."

Commentary: Barry Weyrich found his debut on *Acres of Perhaps* disappointing. In a 1975 interview with *Starlog* magazine, he said, "There was a whole backstory to Mr. Grggit that they didn't film. There'd been an invasion and the alien invaders had realized that the way to control the human populace was through capitalism—they became the owners of companies and used our own greed and conformity against us. When I asked Hugh why he didn't use that stuff, he said, 'We [Jews] have enough trouble already.'"

Night Fever

Charlie could've been out ten years earlier, you know.

There was this guard at Terminal Island, a college guy named Wayne DeVore, and he tried to "rehabilitate us" with his head full of sociology, asking us about our families and how we got there. He had no business being a guard in a federal prison, but that still doesn't mean he deserved what happened to him.

DeVore sometimes patrolled the block by himself at night against regulations just to talk music and philosophy with Charlie, and that's how Billy Hindle got the idea to clock DeVore upside the head with a broken brick to put him to sleep for a couple of hours. It wasn't exactly a well-executed caper or nothing: Billy swung a little too hard and crushed the man's skull into something that looked like a wedge of cheese.

We grabbed the keys and let Charlie out because, after all, he'd been the bait. I wasn't sure how far we'd get with him carrying that fucking guitar, but we made it through six sets of security doors, across the yard, and down to the docks before anybody seemed to notice. It was a terrible storm that night, I remember.

When me and Billy start shucking off our shoes, Charlie looks out over the water and says, "Where's the boat?"

"The boat?" I says. "What boat? We're the boats."

97

Then the siren starts to grind and the footsteps of the guards start to patter in our direction.

Charlie looks at me and then out at the water and then me again and he says, "I can't swim."

Charles Manson can't swim. Who'da thought?

They caught me and Billy three days later in Arizona but they got Charlie right away, standing there on the dock with the guitar on his back, watching us go. They gave him another ten years.

Sometimes I wonder what would be different if Charlie got out when he was supposed to. But then, he'd probably be as big an asshole in the 60s as he was in the 70s.

From *The Making of Charlie: A Prisoner's Testimony*,
by Ronnie Provus (with Veronica Levy).
Farrar and Straus, 1983.

⌘

Yes, Charles Manson's New York of 1977 had its seedy side. When he was released from Danbury Federal Correctional Institution on January 9, Manson rode the bus to a city where 149,000 violent crimes would be committed that year. The so-called Council for Public Safety, comprised of police, firefighters, and other public employees, produced the helpful pamphlet "Welcome to Fear City" to warn tourists away during Mayor Beame's public service cutbacks. There was graffiti and there were muggings and if you saw something called "The Lion King" advertised in Times Square, it wasn't for children.

Yet it's easy to overstate the squalor of the city, exaggerated now for mythic effect and exaggerated then from a fear of the increasing diversity in the streets. If there was graffiti on the subway cars, it was because new voices had something to say. There were new kinds of people loving and living in new kinds of ways. Some of them were doing new and dangerous things.

Some of them were having fun.

From "White Supremacists Can't Dance: The Mediocre Music of Manson," by Leslie Van Houten. *Rolling Stone*, December 1997.

⌘

I came to New York to dance, though not in the way I ended up doing it for Charlie. I started ballet lessons when I was four. My mom drove me the hour south into Indianapolis at least twice a week for twelve years through school for a hundred recitals and fifty performances, not to mention all the classes. Everybody told me I was graceful, beautiful, and amazing, which I believed until about ten minutes after I arrived in New York after high school.

Coming to New York from Indiana is like sailing across the ocean and hitting the Sargasso Sea; it's dense and you slow down, and all you can do is row. I rowed to schools that didn't want me and dance companies that didn't need me. I rowed to jobs at bars and restaurants. I rowed from roommate to roommate, hoping one would make enough for half the rent of a little sixth-floor apartment in the Lower East Side.

The place scared the crap out of me, I'm not going to lie. Everybody makes a big deal out of how dirty it was with everything from newspapers to cars heaped in the streets and under bridges, but what freaked me out the day I arrived was seeing a playground with no grass. None at all. There was a swing set and a merry-go-round, but the ground was just pale cracked pavement. When kids jumped off the swing at the highest it would go, they'd land with this awful "whap!" of their sneakers like someone beating out a carpet.

That's not what playgrounds are supposed to sound like.

Everybody seemed scared or angry all the time, which is really the same thing. That's something Charlie told me, one of the few true things.

I stayed anyway because I thought if I didn't, it was all over for me. My father had picked out the spot where I'd stand behind the counter in his pharmacy for the rest of my life (or until a husband took me home, which he'd have been just as happy with), and I could see it in the linoleum fifty years later on the day I'd die, all worn down to the gray.

I got a job at a bar on Reade Street but I was still auditioning and going to parties where artsy people went. I couldn't get into many of them, but a girlfriend took me to a club called Infinity in the Village, this old envelope factory with columns inside and a giant neon penis on the wall. Sometimes famous people came, she said, and all you had to do while waiting was dance.

So I danced that 4/4 beat through fifty songs a night that all sounded the same. But then there came this...hymn, that's what I'd call it, a hymn. All the nervousness went away and I moved with a powerful abandon I never knew I had in me. It was my song about my life, and it was called was "Dancing Queen."

I know I wasn't the only Dancing Queen in 1977, but it didn't bother me. What I wanted was to be special but part of something, if that makes sense. There was something about the people in that club—like when we all moved at once we didn't have to be scared or angry anymore. Infinity felt like a secret place where we were hiding from the rest (though there were plenty of drug freak outs and bathroom beatdowns).

That's where the idea started in me, the one that Charlie stoked: there were a few people in the world who got it, whatever "it" was, and they had to meet in secret like spies in enemy territory. While the blind dumb zombies marched by on the streets, the Special Ones listened to their tribal music, took their tribal communion, and danced their tribal moves.

Everybody called it disco, but I just thought it was dancing.

> From *Disco Aphrodite: A Manson Girl Speaks Out from Prison*, by Violet "Aphrodite" Wensinger. Doubleday, 1981.

⌘

I'm not going to say that fate set me on a collision course with Charles Manson, but right about the time he was stepping foot in Manhattan, I was returning home from my time in Albany on the Attorney General's staff. Change was in the air, both for the city and my own career.

I'd accepted a position at Peterson, Bryant, & Winter, and in fact, they already had my name plate on a door and a secretary assigned to me, when Robert Morgenthau invited me out for drinks at the Algonquin. I think I'd had two when he asked me to join him in the New York County District Attorney's Office.

I was honored but it was out of the question. "I can't take a demotion like that," I told him.

"It's not a demotion," he said. "You want to make a million dollars in private practice or do you want to be the Mayor of New York someday?"

101

"Can't I do both?" I asked him.

"Don't be such a Republican, Vince," he said.

His ability to make that joke, his attitude that my party didn't matter for the business of the District Attorney's office...that's what sealed the deal.

Eighteen months later, I was prosecuting a disco psychopath cult leader and his followers.

> From *Night Fever: The Story of Charles Manson's Assault on the World*, by Vincenzo Cozzi (with Curt Gentry). W.W. Norton, 1980.

⌘

Certain angry white men like to tell us that the hedonism of disco required a Charles Manson. The idealistic 60s degenerated through drugs and communism to its natural consequences in the Kent State shootings and the riots at the Democratic National Convention. Then came the 70s when we decided that all we could change were ourselves, mostly with crystals and astrology and smooth dance moves. David Bowie's "glitter apocalypse" required horsemen, and those horsemen were Charlie and his Family.

We were frivolous and self-absorbed. A creeping post-war consumerism had led from ranch houses to sequined cowboy boots, and if nothing else, it was a time of enormous advertising efficiency. Millions bought the same pet rocks, wore the same wide collars, danced to the same lyric-less songs, and spoke the same jive.

For these stern judges of culture, we deserved Manson. We summoned him in our club bathrooms through a mirror speckled with cocaine like Bloody Mary.

From "White Supremacists Can't Dance: The Mediocre Music of Manson," by Leslie Van Houten. *Rolling Stone*, December 1997.

⌘

When I wasn't working at the bar or dancing at Infinity, everything seemed cold and shaky. I wasn't doing well at my auditions or meeting anyone in the business. My life was a 12" remix, stretched thin with a throbbing beat that kept me dancing, but the silence between records was terrifying.

One night after work, I was supposed to go to a party in the Upper East Side with some agents and producers around to stare down my dress. I changed in the women's room of the bar and wobbled out to the subway station on my highest heels. When I got to the map, though, I froze. I'm not sure why, but it looked like a bunch of spaghetti all of a sudden and I couldn't make sense of it.

I sat down on a bench, a bad idea at night in those days, and I started to sob. I mean, really sob: like you do when someone dies. I wasn't sure who was dead. Maybe the girl who could have greeted old ladies at her father's drug store. Maybe the one who could have danced at the Met. Or maybe the one who'd get old and leathery serving drinks.

Then I felt this hand on my shoulder and I swung around real fast ready to punch the creep, but it was this little man with a lot of hair and an understanding smile.

"It's okay, baby," he said in a soft voice with a slight Southern accent. "I can't make sense of these trains either."

We both laughed, and I got a longer look at him. He wasn't disco yet but he had tight white slacks and a vest over his bare chest. He wore terrible scuffed white shoes and a brown belt.

"Where you from in Indiana?" he asked.

I was amazed because there's fifty states and he got it on the first guess. As time would go on, I'd believe it wasn't a guess.

"Near Indianapolis," I said.

"Me, too." He held out his hand to me. "They call me Charlie."

When I took his hand, he raised mine to his lips. If anybody else had tried to pull that, I'd have snatched it away, but already I was learning that Charlie had the power to seem innocent and knowing at the same time. If the kiss was a game, it was a game we both knew not to take seriously.

"What did you come here to do?" he asked me. "Everybody comes here to do something."

I started to cry again and he sat down next to me, holding me by the shoulder for at least ten minutes. That's how long it took me to say, "I came here to dance."

"Then dance," he said.

"Where?"

"Everywhere you are, girl," he said.

He wouldn't stop looking at me, waiting, so I stood up and showed him a few of the positions and then a demi-pointe, which is all I could do in my shoes.

"That's incredible," he said, applauding. He stood up and tried the moves himself, tottering on his feet and falling to the pavement.

That night, we made love back at my apartment with my roommates like four feet away. He kissed my toes. Do you know what a ballerina's toes look like? That's what blew me away, what made me think he was Jesus: he loved the ugly in me but didn't think it was ugly.

From *Disco Aphrodite: A Manson Girl Speaks Out from Prison*, by Violet "Aphrodite" Wensinger. Doubleday, 1981.

⌘

At the core, Charlie was a pimp. He was good at it. Not all his followers were as easy to find as Aphrodite Wensinger, but Charlie could see a person's weakness in the worn heels of shoes, in a smudge of mascara, in a crooked hemline. It helped that everybody comes to New York for the same three or four reasons and they (like all of us) think they're unique.

What was horrible about Charlie was that he had an unfailing eye for the dancers, the artists, the writers, the poets: the women who would have some day sung in their own voices instead of his.

Judy "Cookie Puss" Moore, nicknamed from the Carvel ice cream cake TV commercials she found hilarious, came from rural Alabama with three of her plays in a suitcase. Christina "Ziggy" Duffy, an intern at the New York Times for her first summer in the city, was from Marseilles Illinois, a place the residents pronounce "Mar-Sails." Libby "Frodo" Kovacs had run away from her home in Portland, Maine because her psychiatrist father had some strange ideas about sex education. Paula "Princess" Olivolo, Colleen "Velveteen" Pugh, Misty "Slinky" Coleman...they came to be themselves but Charlie made them his.

None of Charlie's women (as he liked to call them and we still unfortunately encourage) were from New York or from other large cities, none were black or Hispanic, none had family nearby, and all felt brave every night they went out. They were brave, which is what Charlie found delicious and nourishing about them.

From "White Supremacists Can't Dance: The
Mediocre Music of Manson," by Leslie Van Houten.
Rolling Stone, December 1997.

⌘

Charlie moved in and I was fine with that. He wasn't making any money but his plans were longer-term than paychecks.

We shared a mattress on the floor in my corner of the apartment and he'd talk all night about where he came from, about his mother trading him to friends for a bottle of liquor and the priests touching him at Boys Town. In the dark, he was honest in a way I never saw again when all the others came along. I guess that's the benefit of being the first girl.

Charlie was worried about my hang ups. He said I was too close to buying into the whole house-in-the-suburbs bullshit story and to help, he brought home a woman he'd met on the NYU campus to live with us and get me out of my ego. She'd been standing on the sidewalk at the site of the Triangle Shirtwaist Factory fire, grinning up at the building with her eyes closed.

Charlie had stood beside her with his arms outstretched and said to her, "Let's catch them."

Her name was Libby Kovacs, though we'd soon start calling her Frodo because she never wore shoes and had weird hairy toes. She wasn't a fan of grooming in general, which I learned that first night when Charlie insisted we had to fully know each other to live as one. He placed tabs of acid on our waiting tongues and choreographed our dance.

Did I want to do it? No, but I wanted to be Charlie's kind of person, someone who'd be willing to do anything that led to life. He'd talked all about how the other people with their mummified hearts stared straight ahead to nothing and I never wanted to be that to him.

Charlie found Sam Englert next and we called him Samson because he was huge and had long hair, plus he had all that Bible stuff swimming in his head. He was sweet, fumbling in bed with us like a boy just out of high school which was what he was. He had a truck, an old Ford with wooden slats on the sides, and that's probably what Charlie saw in him. That and the religious stuff.

I took all three of them to Infinity one night, mostly because I was curious how they'd behave. Libby had been dancing before and she plunged out on the floor like a cop wading into a brawl; she lost her shirt about thirty minutes later and didn't notice. Samson swayed on the floor with girls and some guys flocked all around, pulling on his arms and belt like they were dancing around a maypole.

Charlie...he spent the whole night walking backwards as though trying to get it all into his eyes at once. He watched DJ Ca$hflow at the booth, fascinated by the dual turntables and all the switches and sliders, probably most fascinated by the power: DJ Ca$hflow could make people move and feel as one.

Libby lured Charlie onto the dance floor and showed him her own clumsy moves, but he passed her with his own in about ten minutes. He could flow out there like a cobra rising from a basket, and people kind of backed up in wonder at this guy in an old buckskin jacket strutting like he'd grown up on *Soul Train.*

All he kept saying that night—yelling through the music—was, "Man, where have these people been?"

It was nice to blow his mind for a change.

From *Disco Aphrodite: A Manson Girl Speaks Out from Prison,* by Violet "Aphrodite" Wensinger. Doubleday, 1981.

⌘

Yeah, I remember meeting Charles Manson. It was the single whitest conversation I've ever had.

I'm spinning out "The Hustle" and he's bopping his head along, lurking next to me and watching every move. Dude was a world-class lurker. He had a way of standing right in your blind spot.

He leans in and says, "Is that a synthesizer you think or some guy on a flute?"

He's talking about the music, I realize. The song. All that tootling.

"I got no idea," I tell him.

"Maybe it's a piccolo," he says.

"I don't know what it is, man, but you're standing too close."

He doesn't move. He just says, "Because if that's a piccolo, that brother's really blowing."

That's what Charlie was to us, the kind of white guy who kept a list of jive in his pocket. He carried around that little gun but most of us thought it was a toy, a prop. He seemed goofy and harmless. Like, if the dude came for me in an alley, I was pretty sure I could take him, you know?

> Interview with Marcus "DJ Ca$hflow" McDriscoll.
> "White Supremacists Can't Dance: The Mediocre
> Music of Manson," by Leslie Van Houten. *Rolling Stone*,
> December 1997.

⌘

Q: Ms. Kovacs—

A: Frodo is my true name.

Q: Okay, Frodo: you stayed together in one apartment, is that right?

A: Yeah. It was fun.

Q: How many people lived there?

A: I don't know. About fifteen, coming in and out. We just had pillows and mattresses on the floor. We called it the Safehouse because anybody could come in to get away from whatever—the fuzz, their old men and old ladies, their parents, whatever. You were supposed to bring a little something for everyone to share, a little acid or some weed. We weren't into the heavier stuff, at least not until later when we needed it.

Q: What did you eat?

A: Oh, meals were a big thing for Charlie. We sat in a circle Indian-style and ate whatever we'd found in the trash behind Pathmark. The people in this city think it's garbage but the rest of the world calls it food.

Q: Who found the food?

A: Us girls because we were small and could fit in the Dumpster and the pigs might let us off if we showed them some skin. We cooked it, too, after we got the gas working. We'd let

109

Charlie and the other men eat first because they'd need their strength if the fuzz came down on us.

Q: What music did you listen to in the Safehouse?

A: All sorts of stuff. The record player was going all the time and Charlie'd could come in at any time and wake you up for dancing or sex or dancing and then sex. We had Captain & Tennille, Rod Stewart, ELO, Donna Summer, all the stuff that made you move.

Q: Who decided what to play?

A: Oh, Charlie did. He was the DJ. He knew how music was supposed to flow.

Q: What was his favorite musical group?

A: Hands down, the Bee Gees. He thought they had it all together.

Q: And "Night Fever"...

A: Yeah, he talked about that all the time. We'd have a little communion with acid and trip out on the pillows while he explained what the lyrics meant.

Q: And what did he tell you?

A: It was all about the coming revolution of the kids and the blacks and the gays to overthrow all the old piggy white people. He had every line down, but I can't remember them all.

Q: Well, here, let me show you people's exhibit 219. Does that help?

A: Wow. That's big. You had it printed up. Okay.

Q: These, of course, are the lyrics to "Night Fever." Can you walk us through Charlie's sermon?

A: Well, it starts right there with listening to everything all around you and there's something going down for the young people who can feel it in the streets.

Q: Go on, please.

A: That next part about the waves means the radio, and when they sing about dancing it means people are getting up to take their time on the dance floor. And the part about sharing and stealing means there will be no property after the revolution, everybody sharing, so it won't really be stealing.

Q: Who is the woman controlling his mind and his soul?

A: That's New York, man. It's the rhythm of the city, the beat under your feet, the big disco dance we're all a part of.

Q: And what is it that "we" know how to do in these next lines?

A: It's talking to us, the Family. We know how to do what needs to get done and how to show the world it's time to rise.

Q: And how's that?

A: By killing some of the old white people who were dead already in their paper hearts.

Q: What did the title mean, "Night Fever"?

A: You know what it means. Everybody knows what it means. It's the feeling you get in the night that nothing is wrong and everything's right and it's time to boogie.

Q: Is that what you did at United Nations Plaza with your knives and guns, Miss Kovacs? You "boogied"?

A: Oh, yeah. We boogied.

From *Night Fever: The Story of Charles Manson's Assault on the World,* by Vincenzo Cozzi (with Curt Gentry). W.W. Norton, 1980.

⌘

The media made a big deal out of calling us prostitutes, but to be accurate, we were thieves—nobody intentionally paid us for sex. I know now it's a ridiculous distinction, but Charlie had a way of making the ridiculous sound sane. "No sense makes sense," as he liked to say.

If a man wanted to take us away from Infinity to a hotel room for some sex, then it was our choice to go. If the man was high, it was our job to take care of him. If the man was richer than we were, it was okay to slip a few fifties out of his ostrich-skin wallet for our time because we sure needed them more than he did. And if he was high and tripping, maybe moaning about how his wife wasn't as skinny as we were, it was cool to pick up our shoes and quietly leave.

If someone gave us trouble, there was always Samson to straighten them out.

The only problem was that, as Charlie put it, we were overhunting the preserve. Infinity had a limited clientele, and pretty soon the word was out that money had a habit of disappearing when we were around. The time was coming when they wouldn't let us into the club.

Frodo came up with the solution. One of her "dates" took her to Studio 54 and she saw a whole new world of higher class marks, people who lost ten grand a night up their nose or between the couch cushions. She told us later she watched two girls descending from the ceiling with their legs astride a giant foam unicorn in a rain of glitter, and she knew where we had to be. Where Charlie had to be.

The place had everything she and Charlie loved: celebrities, money, drugs, and plenty of darkness.

From *Disco Aphrodite: A Manson Girl Speaks Out from Prison*, by Violet "Aphrodite" Wensinger. Doubleday, 1981.

⌘

Q: Can you please state your name and occupation for the jury, sir?

A: Steve Rubell, entrepreneur.

Q: What is your most profitable enterprise right now?

A: Right now? Studio 54. You may have heard of it.

Q: And what happens at Studio 54?

A: What doesn't happen at Studio? It's a party with a thousand of my closest friends.

Q: Did you ever see the defendants at Studio 54?

A: A few times, sure.

Q: Do you know the dates?

A: We really don't keep track. I know Charlie started coming around a few months after we opened.

Q: Did you let him in right away?

A: Absolutely not.

Q: Why not?

A: What you have to understand is that I don't run a business. I run a party, and a party is only as good as the people who come. It's a delicate mixture, like baking a cake. Too much of one ingredient, too little of another...suddenly you've got a puddle of batter in your oven. That's my main role at the Studio. I'm like the chef, picking the right ingredients each night. I think you'd be a pretty good ingredient, Mr. Cozzi, like a splash of vanilla.

113

Q: Thank you, Mr. Rubell, but my leisure suit is at the cleaners. I take it Charles Manson was not the right ingredient?

A: Not at first, no. He showed up every night in the same terrible blue suit. His hair and his beard were a mess. He looked like a lost extra from *Planet of the Apes*. He had a good patter, I'll give him that—he was entertaining, talking about his philosophy of disco while I kept pointing to other people over his head.

Q: What changed Manson's fortunes?

A: For one thing, he started dressing like a human being. Someone cleaned him up, trimmed him down to just a moustache, helped him pick out some tighter pants and an open shirt. He had a nice pair of boots that made him taller. And of course, he had the girls with him.

Q: What kind of girls?

A: Cookie Puss, Ziggy, Frodo, Aphrodite, a couple of others. We tried to let them in a few times but they refused without Charlie. Then they'd dance out in the street and they were better than half the people inside. That wasn't good. So they cleaned Charlie up and I finally let him in. That would have been near, what, Thanksgiving of 77, I guess. I was feeling sentimental.

Q: Did you invite him in again after that?

A: Yeah, they were like a circus act. They danced all together and gave out acid. How old fashioned is that, acid? People liked it though and it got them loose and on the floor. They were kind of like unpaid employees. My favorite kind.

Q: Were there any hints of violence?

A: No, but Charlie's big thing was getting in the DJ's booth. He told me all the time about how he had this super power music mix that would blow everyone's minds. I didn't pay much attention, honestly, until he got Truman to talk to me about it.

Q: Truman Capote?

A: Yeah. Charlie had a way of ingratiating himself so most of the guests thought he was just this groovy little guru.

Q: So you gave him a chance as DJ?

114

A: On Truman's suggestion, yes. He said it'd be a "spectacle," that's the word he used. I gave Charlie one hour. Wow, that was the biggest mistake of my life. That hour was death.

From *Night Fever: The Story of Charles Manson's Assault on the World*, by Vincenzo Cozzi (with Curt Gentry). W.W. Norton, 1980.

⌘

The disco scene in New York was one of strange, often literal, bedfellows. For better or worse, Studio 54 was a shimmering beacon of something interesting in New York, something not yet rusty, gray, or abandoned. You'd arrive in your enormous gas-thirsty Chevy with its pressure-cooker engine, and you might be bumping asses with Bella Abzug or David Bowie or Andy Warhol thirty minutes later.

For a brief shining time, it was New York's pacemaker, returning an artificial pulse to a dying city and some dying careers. It was a place to go where you could tell the world— forgive me—that you were staying alive.

The quality or distance of the fame wasn't important; a writer gelded by booze and drugs like Truman Capote could still command an audience because you never knew when he'd be somebody again.

115

From "White Supremacists Can't Dance: The Mediocre Music of Manson," by Leslie Van Houten. *Rolling Stone*, December 1997.

⌘

SCENE: A shark-eyed man wearing two-thirds of a white leisure suit is rapping on my apartment door with a .22 revolver strapped to his hip, and I can't tell if he's here to kill me or screw me.

So I let him in.

I've met Charles Manson in passing at Studio 54, but then, I've met everybody in passing at Studio 54. At Studio, everything is done in passing, and so is everyone. It's possible I've danced with Charlie or his girls, or I've shared a drink with them, or they've offered me something stronger. I may even have taken it.

When Charlie comes into my apartment, he has the bobbing strut of the supple-spined disco man. He lifts his white cowboy boots for step after step across my carpet like a sailor newly back from sea. I motion to the settee and—nodding, smiling humbly—Charlie takes a seat.

Steve Rubell collects people for his club like you or I would collect stamps or coins, and it's clear he has a weakness for the misprints. Charlie is the human equivalent of that stamp with the plane printed upside down, someone who probably shouldn't be but somehow is. He isn't beautiful and he isn't a celebrity, but he is a spectacle, and a club needs those, too.

Manson is even shorter in person than he seems on the dance floor, and here he resembles a little boy sitting uncomfortably on Grandma's couch, afraid to touch the ribbon candy. He is wearing no shirt beneath the jacket of his suit, and the visible stripe of his chest hair looks sweaty as though he's been outside all day playing. At what Charlie plays, I have no idea.

CM: Hey, man, I appreciate you seeing me.

TC: Can I offer you something to drink?

We both glance at the glass bar cart and the glittering skyline of bottles there, but he shakes his head.

CM: I'm not much of a drinker.

TC: Neither am I.

I pour myself my special orange beverage, suspecting I'll need it.

CM: I've seen you at 54 a few times. Everybody loves you.

TC: Do they?

CM: Oh, yeah. They all say you're the guy to talk to, like you know everybody's secrets.

TC: That's not love, Charlie, but sometimes it's good enough.

He's glancing all around now, appraising my home, lingering on the stained glass hanging behind me and the portrait from Warhol.

TC: How long have you been out of prison? Less than a year?

He starts, and for the first time, I see a darkness flash in his eyes that he usually hides better.

CM: Who told you?

TC: You did. I've interviewed a lot of cons, and they all have the wariness you're showing me right now, a kind of defensive bravado. It's a survival mechanism, waking up from your Rip Van Winkle prison dream to a new here and now on the outside.

CM: Prison ain't a dream, brother.

TC: In one way it is—time moves differently there. You learn to adapt, to be tabula rasa, the blank slate ready for whatever culture will have you.

CM: How long have you been out of prison, then?

TC: I'm sorry?

CM: You don't belong on that floor at 54 between Cher and Rocky either, I'll tell you that. You like watching more than dancing.

The vodka is doing nothing for my headache, and neither is Charles Manson. I let the slippers drop and prop my feet on the couch.

TC: Please tell me you have something less obvious to say than that.

CM: How about this: I could kill you if I wanted. This gun is loaded.

TC: I rather wish you would. It does wonders for sales. But I doubt you will. You weren't in prison for murder, I don't think.

CM: You could kill me.

TC: Not on this carpet. Besides, you don't want to kill or be killed. You want, let me guess, to be famous.

CM: Why do you think that?

TC: Because that's why people go to disco clubs, Charlie. It's a very American problem, wanting to belong but be special at the same time. We solve it by becoming celebrities, people who belong at a higher level.

CM: I just want to play my music.

TC: What instrument do you play?

CM: I'm a DJ.

TC: You play other people's music?

CM: When I play it all together, it's my music. I make people feel good, and when I do it right, it changes them.

TC: Into what?

CM: Into people who are turned on. People living in the now, seeing what's what, looking past all the jive and hustle they're being sold.

I sit up again because, truly, this is not a conversation that can be taken lying down anymore.

TC: So you're a disco revolutionary?

CM: Most people call me a disco outlaw, but yeah, I think the world's gonna be real different someday soon and some people are gonna be hurting.

I cover my eyes with my hand.

CM: Are you laughing?

TC: Charlie, you can't be a disco outlaw. The songs are made by companies, the beats calculated by computer. The dances have names, for God's sake—they name the ways you're supposed to move all in unison. The clothes you're wearing, the words you're using...they sold them to you. You bought them.

CM: You don't get it, man. Out there on the floor, we all become one. So what if they sold it to us? That's what the pigs always do, isn't it? They make all the shit we use to take them down. They don't know what they've got so we take it from them. It's Night Fever. We've got it and they don't.

TC: Maybe you are a man of the 70s after all.

CM: Hey, they told me you were cool. That you saw things. I thought you did, too. Aren't you a queer? They're treating you and the blacks and the kids all like shit, like little money batteries, and all you're gonna do about it is write stories?

TC: What did you want me to do? Join your little army?

CM: All I needed was one good word with Steve so I could do my thing. I was gonna go up into that booth and play a music mix that would start something. But maybe you're too old and you've given up.

TC: You want to DJ at Studio? That's your Shot Heard 'Round the World?

119

CM: You'll find out.

I lie back down, this time covering my eyes with a pillow.

TC: If you'd asked nicely, I would have persuaded Steve to let you do it.

There is silence in my apartment though I can feel—almost smell—Charlie standing near me. There is the clicking snap of a holster clasp.

TC: Just not in the face, Charlie.

Again, there is silence.

CM (quietly): I know how the world works.

I feel first a warm hover and then a tugging at my zipper.

From an unpublished essay intended for *Music for Chameleons*, by Truman Capote. 1980.

⌘

Charlie had this idea that the perfect combination of music and drugs could unlock the mass consciousness of all humanity. He called it "Night Fever," and it would turn the whole world into a disco where everybody could dance with everybody and there was nothing but love.

I'm not all sure where he got that idea, but I know he was amazed by how all those random movements on the floor at Studio 54 could seem like one spiritual organism.

120   He worked on the set list for his night at Studio 54 like someone writing an opera. He tested it on us at the Safehouse, playing record after record and watching us make love between them. He tried it with us on MDMA and then with us on speed, and he wove together this magical disco symphony he was sure would change the world.

"We got to be ready," he told us not long before his big debut. There were no lights or music in the Safehouse because the power had been cut off. By then, most of us had been fired from our ordinary jobs, and he'd gotten a few of us gigs as strippers. I'd paid up our account again with money from a private dance, but Con Ed still hadn't gotten around to flipping the switch back on for us.

"How many people in this world do you think are all the way alive?"

We all knew the answer was not many, especially in a city where it was easy to see them all as "traffic."

"Some are kind of alive, some think they're alive enough," he told us, "but they're just running a program they've got from TV and church. Go to work, go home, eat, shit, fuck, buy things. They don't dance. They don't let themselves dance. They're all part of their own hustle."

The thing I see about Charlie now is he rarely said anything untrue—it just wasn't true enough.

"They're not used to being all the way alive. When that mix spreads from the club, it's going to be Night Fever all over the world. The blacks are going to wake up and get theirs, the gays are going to wake up and get theirs, and all the scared white straight people are going to drop to their feet begging to be forgiven."

I remember Frodo squirming on one of the cushions, drizzling wax from a candle in long streaks on her bare legs. "Begging to be forgiven," she said, smiling.

"We're gonna forgive some and we're gonna fuck others, but it's all from love. Some people can't stand being all the way alive so we have to help them."

He took a long-barreled revolver from his jacket and raised it at us. He swept it around the circle and stopped to aim right between my eyes.

"Are you all the way alive, Aphrodite?"

"Yeah," I said.

"Are you alive enough to die?"

"Yeah," I said again.

"Are you alive enough to kill?"

I hesitated then, and Charlie's look could have been disappointment or anger or maybe even fear. By then, he'd taught us those were the same things.

He stood up and then he helped me stand up. He took my right hand and placed the gun there. He placed my finger on the trigger.

"Charlie, I don't—"

"I know," he said. "I know you don't." He knelt before me and positioned the barrel about an inch from his heart.

"Pull the trigger," he said.

My drug of choice was always acid because it made me feel like I could flow through the world like mercury, shimmering and quick. I felt the gun but it seemed far away down my long winding arm, like the signal from my brain would take an hour to get there.

"If you love me, pull the trigger," Charlie said.

"I can't—"

"There's no 'I,'" he said. "There's no 'can't.'"

The thing the counselors keep asking me here in prison is how we could do it. I still don't know, but the closest I come is remembering moments on the dance floor when the music takes you over, when you forget yourself and become something more. There are kinds of music that don't come over speakers but through groups of people, expectations and hopes, tests of love.

I don't know about the others, but I killed for Charlie to prove I was one of the good kinds of people who loved him.

I pulled the trigger. There was a pop, nothing so thunderous as on TV, but Charlie sprawled back with his hands to his heart and blood seeping through his fingers. When he hit the mattress, everybody was leaping and crawling to his side, including me.

The girls started kissing him and so did some of the boys. I patted my way up his body, crying how sorry I was. When I got to his face, I pressed my lips to his. He surged back against me like in the early days, and then he sat up.

Everybody backed away and Charlie opened his hands. A blood-sticky bullet dropped to the floor.

"If you're all the way alive, nothing can hurt you anymore," he said, holding me close.

The lights flickered, surged, and then the record player started to turn. The word "weeeeeee" moaned from the speaker and then "...are family" leaped out at full speed. Everybody started to dance.

At the trial, Cozzi said it had to be a blank, part of Charlie's scheme to make us believers. All I know is that when I opened the cylinder later, the other eight bullets were live.

123

From *Disco Aphrodite: A Manson Girl Speaks Out from Prison*, by Violet "Aphrodite" Wensinger. Doubleday, 1981.

⌘

Yeah, I was there on the night of Charlie's big "debut."

Steve came up to the booth and told me what was going down and promised he'd still pay me. It was annoying, but I figured, okay, fine. Then Charlie shoved me out. I offered to show him how the mixer worked but he shot me this look like it was some kind of insult. I held up my hands and went back with Steve so Charlie could do his thing.

His thing was to lay a big glittering turd on the dance floor.

He had the set list in his shaking hand, and he started off with Meco's Star Wars disco theme because, he told us, "I want to show people they're going to outer space."

That was okay—it was a standard—but then he went down the rest of the list and none of it matched. It was like playing Beethoven with a boxing glove.

See, what people don't know about being a DJ is that it isn't playing music: it's listening to people, feeling them. It's an act of love. You touch the crowd here and see what they do and then you touch them another place. Charlie's set was like bad teenage sex, all about getting him off in the backseat of a car while he pushed and pushed, getting angry when nothing was happening.

I don't remember everything he played, but I know he did "Love Train" and "Shake Your Booty," but he also did "Come Sail Away," which is like undanceable for two full minutes. Two full minutes is an ice age on the floor. It's long enough to kill the dinosaurs.

Everything he played was...ordinary. Stuff you'd hear on the radio. All he had were 45s, no 12 inches, just the canned stuff that people who think they know disco would play. You wouldn't think it was possible to be tone deaf with someone else's music, but Charlie was.

In the end, Charlie got twenty minutes. Truman Fucking Capote was standing in the middle of the lights holding a thumbs down. That's how bad it was.

Steve told a couple of big guys to show Charlie the door, but he didn't go quietly. Neither did the girls or that giant fucking redneck. They were screaming how night fever was coming down fast and all the phonies would be burned alive. Everybody got all quiet and embarrassed for them.

Interview with Xavier "X-Man" Martinez. From "White Supremacists Can't Dance: The Mediocre Music of Manson," by Leslie Van Houten. *Rolling Stone*, December 1997.

⌘

One of the worst ideas I ever had, a blunder that could have cost us the trial, was calling Truman Capote to the stand as a witness. Dave Gerstock and I decided at the end it would look suspicious if none of the putative intended victims of "Night Fever" testified, especially now that all we'd have from Libby Kovacs was her grand jury testimony that Justice Dudley had ruled admissible. Capote was, for better or worse, the sanest person alive who could corroborate Manson's motives.

From the start, though, it was clear Capote was there to entertain himself and needle Manson at every chance.

Probably the most famous example came on the day when I asked Capote why he'd persuaded Steve Rubell to let Charlie DJ at Studio 54.

A: I was curious what he'd do. There was just something fantastic and dangerous about him, that's all.

Q: Attractive?

125

A: Attractive, you mean, to people like me? I suppose he was, in a feral musky sort of way. He seemed wild and strange, like a creature you'd find left on a cottage doorstep in a crib of woven sticks. Feral but...interesting. Like a satyr.

Q: Can you describe a satyr for the jury?

A: I'm sure I don't have to for the jury, but for the lawyers here, I'll say a satyr in the Roman sense was a mythological being with the head and torso of a man but the legs of a goat.

Q: You saw Charles Manson as a satyr?

A: I suppose, though the trouble with Mr. Manson is the goat is his top half.

From *Night Fever: The Story of Charles Manson's Assault on the World*, by Vincenzo Cozzi (with Curt Gentry). W.W. Norton, 1980.

⌘

JUMPIN' JESUS!
Psycho Disco Guru Leaps Eleven Feet to Get at Capote
Tackled by Bailiffs as Girls Chant "Burn Baby Burn!"

From the *New York Post*, April 19, 1979.

⌘

Charlie didn't believe every single person in Studio 54 mocked us as we were taken away—only the famous ones. Just Cher and Andy Warhol and Suzanne Sommers, Rick James and Elton John, and especially Truman Capote.

Things got dark fast after that night. Night Fever was coming down, Charlie assured us, and there were signs of it everywhere. The Blackout last year had been only the start. The lines at the gas stations. Shirtless children climbing all over burned out cars in the Bronx. Son of Sam and the Hillside Strangler and Ted Bundy. Hijackings in the skies. Bombs in the Middle East. People everywhere broke and angry who hadn't yet heard the call of disco.

"When they ain't got nothing more to hustle, they're gonna come hustle us," is what he kept saying.

Guns aren't hard to come by in New York and Charlie became a collector. The Safehouse started looking less like the harem room of an Arab potentate and more like an armory. Charlie and Samson traded drugs and sex with us for machine guns and swords and bayonets, and pretty soon they were cleaning them night and day with "Night Fever" warbling over and over from the record player.

They taught us how to use them, and I guess the smallest part of me, the Indiana part, knew that when we did, it wouldn't be good. I wish I could say I was a better person, the one my parents raised, but I guess when you hear and see the same things every day and only those things over and over, you do what the rest of the monkeys are doing.

I'm sorry that's all the explanation I have.

From *Disco Aphrodite: A Manson Girl Speaks Out from Prison*, by Violet "Aphrodite" Wensinger. Doubleday, 1981.

⌘

Q: Okay, Ms. Wensinger, if you're ready, please tell us what happened on the night of November 19th last year.

A: Charlie didn't let us keep up with the news, but we had a radio. Between all the songs, they came on with this story about these people who'd killed themselves in South America.

Q: At Jonestown in Guyana?

A: Yeah, but we were hazy on the details. By then, we were all on speed for most of the nights and half of the days because Charlie wanted us alert for whatever came down. That's what came down.

Q: The murder-suicide of more than 900 followers of Reverend James Warren Jones.

A: Back then, they were saying it was a few hundred.

Q: What was Charlie's reaction?

A: He took it as a sign.

Q: Of what?

A: That Night Fever was starting. He had this vague idea they were all black and Communist and they liked to dance.

Q: He was inspired by Jones?

A: You know, I'm not so sure. I think in the end he was jealous of him. That he'd talked so many people into dying for him. All Charlie had was about ten of us.

Q: What did he do?

A: He turned off the radio and told us it was time. We had to get on the revolution's dance floor and show our moves.

Q: What was the plan?

128

A: The basic gist was he wanted us to kill as many famous people in New York as quickly as we could. He joked about how many it would take to steal the headlines from Jones, what the exchange rate was between a rich white person and a bunch of broke black ones.

Q: What did he have you do?

A: He told us to get into dark clothes and then go with Samson and Frodo down to U.N. Plaza to get Truman Capote.

Q: What did he mean by "get"? Do you remember his exact words?

A: He said, 'Write his last story for him.'

Q: What was he going to do while you were doing that?

A: He was going to take Cookie Puss and Ziggy to get John Lennon.

Q: After you "got" Capote, what were you supposed to do?

A: After Capote, we were supposed to get Barry Manilow, and after Lennon, they were supposed to get Andy Warhol.

Q: Did anybody protest or disagree?

A: No. Frodo was stomping all around like Godzilla, roaring.

Q: How did you feel?

A: I was scared. Not of doing it so much as of what was waiting for us down in the streets. Charlie had made it seem like the whole world would be like the blackout again, smashing windows and beating people in the streets with pipes.

Q: How were you armed?

A: He gave me this crazy long bayonet that hung from a belt and Samson had a couple of Buck knives and a rifle, and I think Frodo had a hammer or something.

Q: What were your orders?

A: He took me aside and told me I was the smart one, the one he trusted and loved the most. He told me I knew what had to be done, that it had to be special.

Q: Do you remember the word he used?

A: Yes. He said to make it 'witchy.'

129

From *Night Fever: The Story of Charles Manson's Assault on the World*, by Vincenzo Cozzi (with Curt Gentry). W.W. Norton, 1980.

⌘

Samson parked his truck on 49th Street in front of 860 U.N. Plaza. The wheels popped up on the curb and we probably looked like a murderous version of the Beverly Hillbillies, Samson shirtless in his overalls. The doorman rushed at us in his uniform with the big gold epaulets and Samson jumped down from the driver's seat. Frodo sprung from the passenger side and I was still climbing out when I heard Samson's whooping noise and then the crack of gunshots.

All I saw across my eyes was the color red.

I stumbled on the concrete for some reason and fell right next to the doorman, whose name I now know is Devi Ibrahim. Blood was bubbling from a large hole in the center of his face, and something like words were whistling from somewhere in that skull like air was leaking from everywhere. My face was inches from his and I think he saw me. I hope I didn't look scary in the last moments of his life but I probably did. Everybody's scary when you're dying.

"I'm sorry," I said.

I followed Frodo and Samson into the lobby, and I saw Samson poking the rifle barrel between the closing elevator doors. I saw three, four flashes in the crack of the doors, and then there was a ding when they opened again. Frodo skipped inside with her hammer raised, and the man we found wounded in the corner was holding up his hands and crying out, "Wait! Do you know who I am?"

"You're dead," Frodo said, swinging the hammer. It cracked against his arm, the left ulna as they said in court, and his scream went around and around us in the elevator like a pinball. Samson was pressing the button for the 23rd floor and letting Frodo take care of business.

"I'm the Deputy—"

She swung lower this time, catching the man under the jaw. Teeth flew from his mouth as Samson watched with smiling approval.

"—Permanent—"

That was Timothy Surgeoner's last word. She slammed the hammer down on the top of his head and it sank nearly to his nose. We didn't find out until later he was America's Deputy Permanent Representative to the United Nations, on his way home from the office. Frodo stomped his briefcase, laughing because it was Samsonite.

Everything was still red.

The elevator doors opened on the 23rd floor to a very surprised married couple, the Auldridges. We had no way to know he'd been a Green Beret in Vietnam, but he shoved his wife aside and stormed toward Samson, who hadn't been expecting it. They fell back into the elevator and Mr. Auldridge had his thumb stuck deeply into Samson's neck.

Frodo took the bayonet from my belt and put it in my hands. "Do it to it!" she said.

I looked down. Samson's eyes were bulging, something that terrified me to see in someone I'd slept with, someone I'd loved. Yet even then I hesitated.

Frodo wrapped her hands around mine, sticky with someone's blood, and she guided the bayonet into the center of Chip Auldridge's back. He lifted his head and cried out, but

131

then Samson threw him off. I kept stabbing because he was there and he was already dead and if I was stabbing, maybe they wouldn't make me do anything else.

Frodo sang out a few bars of "Stayin' Alive" in time with my motions, but then she ran into the hallway calling out, "Where ya goin', tiny dancer?" She caught up to Mrs. Auldridge by plunging the hammer claw between her shoulder blades.

The building seemed to list to one side when I stood up, and at the end of the hallway, I saw Samson kicking at a door. It took him two tries before splintering under the force of his foot. The two of them ran in and I staggered after, which is how my handprint got on the wallpaper. I didn't do it on purpose. I didn't do it to be witchy.

Samson and Frodo were screaming in the apartment, tearing it apart in a real helter skelter, smashing the stained-glass pictures and stabbing the couches and tearing books in half at the spines. Capote wasn't home, but they chopped or slashed their way into every closet and cabinet to be sure. Frodo threw a typewriter through the window and it tumbled to the street below, and then she threw a bunch of manuscript pages after it, something Cozzi later said was a book called *Answered Prayers*. It fluttered out the window like a flock of pigeons.

Answered Prayers. When I looked it up, I found out that's from a quote saying answered prayers are more painful than the unanswered ones.

Before we left the apartment, Frodo leaped up onto the bed, lifted up her skirt, and left a huge shit in the middle of the pillow. Then she wrote "BURN THIS MUTHA DOWN" and "DO IT TO IT" and "NIGHT FEVA" in blood on every wall we could find. I was the one who wrote "WE ARE FAMILY" in the elevator.

From *Disco Aphrodite: A Manson Girl Speaks Out from Prison*, by Violet "Aphrodite" Wensinger. Doubleday, 1981.

⌘

While Sam, Libby, and Violet were assaulting 860 U.N. Plaza, Charles Manson was calmly driving through the city in a stolen Chrysler like a tourist dad with his daughters. He was somehow unable to find the enormous section of trees and grass on an island and follow it around until sighting one of the most famous buildings in the world.

Manson couldn't—or, more likely, didn't want to—find the Dakota. For Cozzi at trial, this meant he was more interested in his own animosities than starting Night Fever, and maybe that was true. For a lot of others, it meant he was a chicken shit, and that was true, too.

They gave up after an hour and he took them for ice cream.

From "White Supremacists Can't Dance: The Mediocre Music of Manson," by Leslie Van Houten. *Rolling Stone*, December 1997.

⌘

When Jurors Three and Eleven returned, I asked if they needed anything and they shook their heads. I could tell from their pallor and the sweat beading on their foreheads that they wanted it over as quickly as possible and I felt it was my duty to oblige. By then, five hours into Violet Wensinger's testimony, I wanted it to be over, too.

Q: What happened when you reached the ground floor?

A: When the doors opened, there was an old lady standing there with one of those folding carts full of groceries.

133

Q: Deborah Lunt?

A: That turned out to be her name, yes.

Q: What happened?

A: She looked at us all soaked in blood, Samson with the rifle in his hand and Frodo with my bayonet. I was flexing my fingers because the blood was drying on my skin and making them stiff. That's a funny thing to remember, but I do.

Q: How did Mrs. Lunt react?

A: She started cursing at us. "Get the fuck outta here! This is a nice neighborhood!" Then Samson raised the rifle under her chin and fired once. Her hair blew up into the air.

Q: What was Ms. Kovac doing?

A: By then, half the building had called the cops and one was just arriving. He got out of the car with his pistol drawn, and Frodo ran to him screaming, "Murder! Murder!"

Q: Sergeant Steve Robey?

A: Yes. That's who it was.

Q: How did he react to Ms. Kovac?

A: He looked Frodo over and held out his other arm. He was saying, "It's okay, honey, I got ya" when she swung the bayonet and nearly decapitated him.

From *Night Fever: The Story of Charles Manson's Assault on the World*, by Vincenzo Cozzi (with Curt Gentry). W.W. Norton, 1980.

⌘

SIX KILLED IN U.N. SLAYFEST
Giant Assailant Nearly Shrugs Off Four U.N. Cops
Giggling Girl Accomplices Covered in Blood

From the *New York Post*, November 20, 1978.

⌘

By the following Wednesday morning, the attacks at the U.N. had been digested and excreted by the media, and the alleged assailants were already famous for their cheerful disregard for the seriousness of their situation.

They'd been caught literally red-handed. There were bloody finger- and footprints all over the scene, not to mention enormous handwriting exemplars on the walls. They'd been seen by two dozen witnesses. The police had seized Violet Wensinger's bent bayonet, Libby Kovacs's Buck knife and claw hammer, and Sam Englert's .30-06 semi-automatic rifle. There was a sawed-off shotgun in the truck.

I remember tucking the New York Times under my arm in the elevator on the way to my office and thinking a few public defenders were about to have a very bad Thanksgiving.

Then Robert Morgenthau called me into his office.

"Did you hear about this U.N. thing?"

I told him I had. "Those kids are in big trouble," I added.

"Yes," he said. "They're in trouble with us. It's your case."

That made no sense. "Isn't one of the victims the deputy ambassador? Wouldn't that be a federal case?"

"There's some ambiguity there, it seems. The State Department wants us to take it. Something about how they'd prefer this to seem like a problem with dirty old New York instead of the whole country. Plus if you blow it, they get another shot with federal charges."

"What's to blow? They'd have to be crazy not to plea out."

"Funny you should say that," Morgenthau said, handing me the first of ten thousand files we'd gather on the case.

135

From *Night Fever: The Story of Charles Manson's Assault on the World*, by Vincenzo Cozzi (with Curt Gentry). W.W. Norton, 1980.

⌘

Charlie didn't read books all the way through, but he sure had a knack for finding the one or two things he could use from them, just like he did with people. One of his favorites was *Illusions*, by the same guy who wrote the one about the seagull. What Charlie took from it was that we create the world around us, and I'm not responsible for the world you're creating around you.

"Life is an illusion, death is an illusion, money is an illusion. We make it all up to test ourselves, and if you're bent out of shape by someone else's illusion, you better check your own," he told us once.

Rikers Island was no illusion, and Charlie's absence from the visiting room was no illusion either. I was scared to death, and I had two things to hold onto: Frodo and a line from *Illusions* that went, "Laughing on the way to your execution is not generally understood by less-advanced life-forms, and they'll call you crazy." So that's why I laughed as much as I did for the cameras. That's why I stared. That's why I sang stupid songs. That's why I held up my bloody hands in their cuffs and licked them.

I thought if everyone thought I was crazy, it meant I was really being brave.

From *Disco Aphrodite: A Manson Girl Speaks Out from Prison*, by Violet "Aphrodite" Wensinger. Doubleday, 1981.

⌘

CHARLIE'S DEMONS
Slay Cult Girls Sing "You Light Up My Life" at Arraignment
Kovacs Claims Mysterious Man Will Save Them

From the *New York Post*, November 22, 1978.

⌘

Samuel Paul Englert, AKA Sam Englert, AKA Samson, wasn't a docile prisoner. His long descent from his cocktail of drugs back to reality made him scream, shudder, and sweat so much that corrections officers had a hard time containing him. When they brought him to the mental health unit, he put his hands behind his head as though relaxing, just to show how he'd broken the cuffs hours ago.

Englert's father, the pastor of the largest televised Sunday service in South Carolina, sent an attorney on a chartered jet within an hour of his son's arrest. My interview with Sam at Rikers was four words.

Q: Hello, I'm—

A: Lawyer's coming.

Elizabeth Mary Kovacs, AKA Libby Kovacs, AKA Frodo, was the most annoying prisoner ever contained in Rikers Island, which is saying something. She sang songs endlessly, mostly "We Are Family" and "Love Will Keep Us Together." She sometimes stopped in the middle of whatever she was doing to show off a few disco moves, her shackles and handcuffs jangling. She flirted with the guards whatever their gender. She made lewd gestures and comments. She could make a continuous shrieking noise that seemed to come from

137

a set of bottomless lungs. She sometimes spoke in tongues and gave four different names at her booking, including "Mary Magdalene," "Eva Braun," and "Freya Jackalsdottir."

We later discovered this was Charlie's coaching: the best way to confound the authorities was to appear crazy. When I tried to interview her, she was in rare form.

Q: Hello, Libby. I'm Vince Cozzi from the DA's office. This is Detective Kirchner.

A: Crack the case yet? I think those kids you arrested might be dangerous.

Q: You're from Maine, aren't you? Somewhere near Portland?

A: I'm from everywhere. I'm from inside you.

Q: But mostly from Maine, right? The reason I'm asking—

A: The rain in Maine stays plainly in the brain.

Q: —is that we can contact your family for you if you'd like.

A: Wonderful. Dad would be pleased I've gotten better at hand jobs than when I was six.

Q: Libby, if you're the victim of a crime, we can have that looked into for you. But right now, you're the perpetrator of one and we both know you aren't crazy. An insanity plea is very difficult to prove, and if your lawyer suggests one, I'd caution you to reconsider. The best thing you can do now is help Detective Kirchner and me to understand what happened in your own words.

A: Frap frap. Meowly derg.

Q: What is that?

A: Those are my own words.

Q: This isn't a game, Ms. Kovacs.

A: It will be when Charlie gets here.

138

Violet June Wensinger, AKA Violet Beauregard, AKA Aphrodite, was quieter than Libby but by no means silent. She sang in ragged harmony with her co-defendant, though she rarely finished a whole song. The expression in her mugshot is so dead that many of the guards later said she was the creepiest of the bunch, shut off from the world.

Q: Ms. Wensinger, I'm Vince Cozzi. This is Detective Sean Kirchner. We're here to talk to you about the other night.

A: My lawyer hasn't come yet.

Q: Well, you don't have to talk to us, but it would—

A: I hope he brings me something to drink.

Q: You want something to drink? We can get you something. There's a machine outside. What's your favorite?

To this day, I'm not sure why I used that word, a child's word. Maybe there was something child-like about her. Maybe I was only hoping.

A: My favorite? You're asking me what my favorite is?

Q: Yeah, what do you want?

A: I killed a person and you're going to buy me my favorite? That's how I accidentally won the trust of our star witness.

From *Night Fever: The Story of Charles Manson's Assault on the World*, by Vincenzo Cozzi (with Curt Gentry). W.W. Norton, 1980.

139

⌘

I'd seen Charlie do magical things, not just recovering from that bullet. He could soothe pigeons in his hands and jump out of the way of traffic just in time. He could look into anyone's heart, I thought, and he once stooped beside a blind beggar on the corner, held the man's face in his hands, and said,

"Brother, you can see again." The man walked away without his cane.

I imagined Charlie drifting across the East River to Rikers like all those illustrations of Jesus after the resurrection in my children's Bible. His hands would be open at his sides, and there'd be a serene expression on his face. The bars would peel back like shriveling weeds and the stone would crumble to dust.

None of that happened. One day passed and then another, and Charlie didn't come for us. John Lennon was still alive and so was Andy Warhol, and nobody was strutting in the streets. Nothing was different. That's what scared me the most: killing six people didn't knock the whole Earth off its axis.

> From *Disco Aphrodite: A Manson Girl Speaks Out from
> Prison*, by Violet "Aphrodite" Wensinger.
> Doubleday, 1981.

⌘

It had to be frustrating for Charles Manson to be free while his followers became more famous than he was, their faces on TV and their words—his on loan to them—in the papers. A true revolutionary, the Che Guevara of the dance floor, might have declared himself with something big, a dramatic show of his deadly fervor. His natural cowardice and his ex-con's skill for lying low won out in the end, and he sent Cookie Puss and Ziggy to do it instead.

On December 9, he sent Judy Moore and Christina Duffy to rent a U-Haul with a stolen credit card at Flatbush. Cookie Puss's main qualification for the job was she could drive a stick shift, albeit poorly. Bill DeJardins, the rental clerk, winced as they lurched away with the grinding of gears. He recalled she was driving barefoot.

Their next stop was Dyno Fuel Oil where they bought five fifty-gallon drums of kerosene. Thuan Ngoc, sworn in as an American eighteen months earlier, wasn't sure if it was suspicious for two girls to be buying so much, and he was skeptical of their story that they were stocking up for winter. He balked briefly, but then Ziggy told him (honestly) their boyfriend would be very upset if they didn't come home with it. He made the sale.

Somewhere in an alley, Manson and his followers covered the panels of the truck with black house paint and wrote their magic words on the sides: DO IT TO IT, NIGHT FEVA, BURN THE MUTHA DOWN. They drew stars and moons on it, too, for luck.

At 11:24, the truck slowed to a stop in front of Studio 54. There was still a crowd waiting to get in even with the cold, and Steve Rubell was choosing his second wave of guests for the night.

When he saw the truck, he shouted, "If that thing isn't full of bare asses, get it the fuck out of here!"

Cookie Puss jumped out of the passenger door, grinning and waving like a celebrity. She had a bottle of vodka in her hand.

141

From *Night Fever: The Story of Charles Manson's Assault on the World*, by Vincenzo Cozzi (with Curt Gentry). W.W. Norton, 1980.

⌘

When we saw two of Manson's chicks get out all dressed in black, everybody was like, "These assholes again?"

They all saw the bottle but I saw the rag in the top, and when she flipped open the old Army Zippo, I knew shit was going down. I grabbed the girl I was trying to get into the club and faced her toward the wall with my back to the truck, and there was this big warm wave that rolled over all of us. People started screaming.

She doesn't tell the story, but the girl was one I'd met at Dunkin Donuts named Madonna Ciccone.

Interview with Xavier "X-Man" Martinez. From "White Supremacists Can't Dance: The Mediocre Music of Manson," by Leslie Van Houten. *Rolling Stone*, December 1997.

⌘

DISCO INFERNO
Studio 54 Seared By Fire, 65 to Hospital with Burns
Two Assailants Dead; Possible Connection to U.N. Slay

From the *New York Post*, December 10, 1978.

⌘

Charles Manson didn't expect there to be survivors of his truck bomb attack on Studio 54, and there might not have been if he'd remembered a key ingredient lost somewhere in his street explosives lore: fertilizer. Without it, the truck burst into flame and blew apart, but the only victims standing close enough to be swallowed wholly by the flames were Judy Moore and Christina Duffy.

Witnesses said they didn't even run. NYPD found Duffy's distinctive dental bridge from an ice skating accident in what was left of her blackened skull.

The many wounded were taken to Presbyterian, and the ones who could talk told detectives only a first name: Charlie. It was Steve Rubell, seated on a gurney without hair or eyebrows, who grabbed a uniformed officer by the collar and said, "His last name is Manson. It's Charles Mother Fuckin' Manson."

From *Night Fever: The Story of Charles Manson's Assault on the World*, by Vincenzo Cozzi (with Curt Gentry). W.W. Norton, 1980.

⌘

They did their best to keep us from talking to each other at Rikers, but Frodo got a message to me through a line of other prisoners. It came in a crossword puzzle from the paper, and it said, "Have faith in you and the things we do," which was one of Charlie's ways of telling us to keep our mouths shut when shit hit the fan, especially around cops. I'd been doing just that, no matter how nice Cozzi was to me.

It was a relief to hear from someone. After days and days, how many I couldn't tell, and nobody had come to visit me. No Charlie, no Cookie Puss, no Ziggy. I had to learn why from a newspaper.

143

When I saw the *Post* with those pictures on the front page of stark white blankets over the only two corpses, I doubled over in my cell and threw up. It wasn't the first time I'd done that in jail by then, but this time it didn't seem to stop. It kept going and going until my stomach had nothing more, but even then, it surged like it wanted to come out, too.

To the world today, Cookie Puss was a crazy girl who died with her hand melted into the hand of another crazy girl, but to me, she was an almost miraculous friend, the one who taught me how to be a woman of the 70s instead of the 50s like my mother wanted. She took me to get birth control. She read me her plays, funny ones about people who found their own kind of love. She taught me how to say no to every man but Charlie.

If I'd met her first, I might not even have needed him.

Ziggy I didn't know as well because she was the quiet observant type. Most people don't know this, but she had one of those perfect memories; she could tell you the last thirty license plates she'd seen. She saw a lot more than most of us, and sometimes I think she just got all filled up with that pain and had nowhere to put it.

It's funny the things you can think when there isn't someone else's beat in your heart. What I noticed most about those days was Charlie's silence. When we killed those six people at U.N. Plaza, he said nothing. When John Lennon didn't end up dead, he said nothing. When Cookie Puss and Ziggy burned, still nothing. For once, he wasn't everywhere—he was nowhere. He was the Nowhere Man, like all the others who disappear when the rent needs to be paid or a period doesn't come, as mine hadn't since my arrest.

An emotion crept back inside me, one whose name I'd forgotten because only Charlie was allowed to feel it. Anger.

When Cozzi came for another of his visits later that night, he looked as though he hadn't slept in about thirty-six hours. He wasn't even wearing a tie.

"I won't waste time with you, Violet. You're the smartest one of the bunch. Is Charlie's last name Manson?"

"Yes," I said. The world should know his name.

"We're going to find him, Violet," Cozzi said, switching to a seat closer to mine at the interrogation table. "The difference is whether we find him by our surprise or his. If it's ours, a lot more people could get killed."

"If it's his, it'll be him?" I asked.

"We don't want that to happen," Cozzi said.

I never knew the Bible as well as Charlie and Samson did; my faith was the Vacation Bible School kind, all songs about Zacchaeus and not keeping your light under a bushel. I did know the story of Judas, though, and Charlie told us once he was the hero of the whole Bible. He was the guy, after all, who made Jesus famous.

I said, "He's hiding in the walls."

> From *Disco Aphrodite: A Manson Girl Speaks Out from Prison*, by Violet "Aphrodite" Wensinger.
> Doubleday, 1981.

⌘

The lease had long lapsed on the so-called Safehouse, and the Family's solution to this problem was novel, if terrifying. They simply slithered into the walls and maintenance areas like cockroaches, creating secret doors into every apartment where they helped themselves to food and cash (and the occasional nap or lay in a clean bed) with the residents seldom the wiser.

If you were a child in that building from 1978 to 1979 and saw a hairy monster in your closet, there's a good chance that monster was Charles Manson.

This made the tactical situation difficult for NYPD officers but not impossible. They stormed the building of the Safehouse with their revolvers and shotguns drawn, and in Violet's old apartment, they found a removable closet panel leading into the darkness. They chased a half dozen barefoot people to ground, ducking under rusted pipes and jumping over heaps of trash. Princess, Velveteen, and Slinky made it as far as the fire escape but no farther.

Officers did a floor-by-floor sweep of the building and might have never found Manson if Officer DePaoli hadn't seen two sets of four filthy fingertips poking out from the top of the garbage chute. He motioned with the barrel of his gun and two other policemen took up positions at the sides.

"If it was up to me, I'd have crushed that dickhead's fingers and let him slide down into the goddamned furnace," DePaoli told me in his pre-trial interview. "But fuck it all, we're supposed to be the good guys."

Inside the chute they found a mop of greasy hair. DePaoli grabbed it and the face underneath grinned up at him like a child playing hide and seek.

"It's okay, brother," Charles Manson told him, laughing.

"It's everything but okay, shithead," replied DePaoli.

From *Night Fever: The Story of Charles Manson's Assault on the World*, by Vincenzo Cozzi (with Curt Gentry). W.W. Norton, 1980.

⌘

Charlie sauntered past the news cameras in his disco cowboy suit all covered in soot, but the holster was empty. He was mugging for the reporters, answering some of their questions with his little reflection trick.

"Why'd you do it, Charlie?"

"Why'd you make me do it, brother? Why'd you kill all the whales and keep your kids in your prison-schools? Why'd you send all them little brown people to heaven from Vietnam? I did it because you did it."

"Why Studio 54?" cried another.

"Why? Why is a lie, woman. There is no why. There's only Is. They all deserved to dance in the sky." Then he turned to the camera and said, "Stay tuned after these messages, home audience, because there's gonna be more!"

That was the start of Charlie's dark magic for the rest of the world, the reason every newspaper from Tokyo to Berlin came to cover the trial, the cause of a sharp spike in the sales of guns and guard dogs. He had the power to make you a celebrity just by killing you, and in the dark corner of too many gawkers' hearts, it'd be worth it.

> From "White Supremacists Can't Dance: The Mediocre Music of Manson," by Leslie Van Houten. *Rolling Stone*, December 1997.

⌘

By himself away from the cameras, Charles Manson was downright obsequious to authority. He said "sir" and "ma'am" to the guards and joked with them amiably. He saved the wide-eyed declarations of race and class warfare for the media.

I went to see him as soon as I could, and from the moment I did, he asked me to call him Charlie. That was nice, seeing as how we'd be colleagues for the next eight months.

"I'm Vince Cozzi from the DA's office," I told him, in case he thought I was his public defender.

"Yeah, I know who you are. You're doing a great job."

"Thanks. You know I'm trying to put you and the others away in Sing Sing for the rest of your lives, right?"

Charlie shrugged. "What's another prison, man? I've been in them all my life. I like the one with the sky above it better, but sometimes that sky gets scary. That sky looks at you."

"You could save the state a lot of money by pleading guilty, you know," I said.

He grinned. "Then I wouldn't have my say."

"I've talked to Violet. She's been having your say."

"What's that crazy bitch been saying?"

"She says you're trying to start a revolution with disco. You call it 'Night Fever,' and once all the people rise against the squares, you'll take command of them all."

"First of all," he said, "nobody calls them squares anymore except for squares. Second of all, that's Violet's trip, man, not mine. It's the kids who are having this revolution, not me. I'm just showing them the way because nobody else will."

"There are eight dead people and sixty-five wounded," I said. "You're still nine hundred short."

His amiable smile faltered. "Nine hundred short?"

"Of Jim Jones. You should have waited a year or so, Charlie, because now you won't even be remembered in his shadow."

"You got a funny way of asking a brother to plea out," Manson said.

"I know you're not going to plea out," I said. "But what I don't get, Charlie, is why you'd think attacking a disco club would make the people inside join you instead of hate you. Unless you thought they already did."

148

He opened his hands and spread them wide as though to say he contained multitudes.

From *Night Fever: The Story of Charles Manson's Assault on the World*, by Vincenzo Cozzi (with Curt Gentry). W.W. Norton, 1980.

⌘

"JESUS HAD NO LAWYER"
Manson to Serve as Own Attorney
Fires Third Public Defender

From the *New York Post*, February 17, 1979.

⌘

DISCONSPIRACY
Murders, Arson to Be Tried as Continuous Crime
Manson Agrees to Cozzi Motion

From the *New York Post*, February 21, 1979.

⌘

Charles Manson did his best for nearly four months to disrupt the court, instructing his followers to scream at Justice Dudley, to turn their backs to the flag, to chant their songs. He leaped out for Capote when he was on the stand. He drew his finger across his throat when Violet Wensinger took the stand.

"Your world is jive!" he screamed once when Justice Dudley overruled one of his many frivolous objections. "Don't you understand, brother? You of all people?"

149

Justice Dudley, who is African-American, had Manson removed from the courtroom. When the girls and Samson started to shout, "Your world is jive!", he had them removed, too.

Manson's antics drew a few dozen malcontented teenagers in front of 60 Centre Street with the last remaining free Family members, led by Velveteen Pugh. At night they giggled and slept in a ragged camp of old Boy Scout tents. During the day, they threatened reporters and looky-loos with the coming disco apocalypse.

"The spirit you judge is your own," Velveteen told one tourist from Seoul. "You hate his hustle because you hate your own."

There was a certain desultory spirit to their declarations, though, and the cuffs of their yellowing satin pants were frayed. In the light, the missing sequins and safety pins were all too apparent, and their faith was dying out under the sun as surely as Manson was dying in the courtroom.

> From "White Supremacists Can't Dance: The
> Mediocre Music of Manson," by Leslie Van Houten.
> *Rolling Stone*, December 1997.

⌘

150   On June 27, 1979, the People rested.

We'd called 64 witnesses, introduced 119 pieces of evidence including a four-by-four foot section of Truman Capote's wall, and racked up 14,000 pages of court transcript. We had fingerprints from Englert, Kovacs, and Wensinger at the scene. We had handwriting experts identify the writing on the wall with a 75% certainty, not great but at least circumstantial. We'd undermined the diminished capacity defense with psychiatric examinations of all suspects but Charlie, who refused.

Charles Manson had objected to testimony 1,455 times. Of those, 85 were sustained.

The next day, Justice Dudley asked Manson to call his first witness.

"I've got one, your honor," he said. "Me."

"Very well, Mr. Manson."

Charlie sheepishly rubbed his hand in his hair. "Do I ask myself a question in one voice and then answer it in another?"

"That's not necessary. When you take the stand, you can give Mr. Sivasco the questions you want to answer."

Greg Sivasco, Manson's "consulting" public defender, will one day be remembered as a saint of the criminal justice system. Manson had taken almost none of his advice and demanded he be removed more than once. Members of the Family had snuck into his apartment and moved the furniture around before leaving a bullet on his pillow.

Greg handed Charlie a yellow legal pad and Manson wrote a single question on it.

Charlie placed his hand on the Bible and swore he'd tell the truth. Then he sat down and Greg, sighing, approached with the legal pad.

"Mr. Manson," he said, "Can you tell us what it's all about?"

Justice Dudley glanced toward me, expecting me to object to such a broad question. I didn't because I wanted Manson to have all the rope he needed.

"I was born to a whore in Cincinnati," he began. "I never knew my father, and so the system became my father. I've spent most of my life in your jails, sometimes the ones with bars and sometimes the ones you live in with paychecks and timecards."

If Manson had ever gotten a paycheck, I'd found no evidence of it.

"I've wanted one thing my whole life, to be free. I've been free in my head but not free in my body, but when I got out a couple years ago, I saw some people had figured it all out. They wore crazy clothes and they talked about love, and you'd done your best to put away the people like that in the Sixties but all you'd done was drive them into the darkness where they belonged. They were my people, and I came home to claim them.

"They were all about love, just like I'm all about love. I love people enough to free them from the life your system has made for them. Everything hateful you've said about me is your own reflection. I'm your mirror, your garbage dump mirror, where you throw all the things you don't want to see in yourselves.

"Did those kids kill because they love me? I don't know. But I do know our country kills people all the time without loving them.

"Mr. Cozzi's given us a fair trial, as fair as he could anyway, but he's all wrong about Night Fever. It's not murder. It's love. It's about the people who have so much love inside that they have to dance, and it's about the terrible people who've given up on dancing who want to stop them.

"It's an ugly time, brothers and sisters, an ugly time. In an ugly time, people don't know what's beautiful. You don't know the music that's beautiful. You don't know the clothes that are beautiful. You don't know the people who are beautiful because if you do, you got to know you're ugly.

"None of us killed nobody. The 70s killed them and maybe it was us who were the hands, I don't know. All I know is I'm the trashman who picked up the kids you threw away, and you will do with me as you will, as you always have."

"Are you concluded, Mr. Manson?" Justice Dudley asked.

"I am concluded."

"Mr. Cozzi, your cross?"

In my briefcase, I had a spiral notebook of questions for Charles Manson, catching him in any of a thousand lies and inconsistencies, peeling back the gilding of religious philosophy he'd painted on his selfish desire to kill the people who'd rejected him, their rightful master. I could have kept him up there another three months.

But the truth is I was tired. Justice Dudley was tired, the jurors were tired, the reporters were tired. We were tired of watching this performance and we wanted it to be over, me most of all.

"One question, Charlie," I said.

He looked surprised. He'd wanted to spar with me, his nemesis, the black knight of the straight world.

"Your sentence in federal prison was ten years longer than it had to be, thanks to your botched escape attempt. If you'd gotten out in 1967 instead of 1977, do you think the kids you 'picked up' then would have killed anybody?"

Throughout the trial, I avoided any appearance of taking advantage of Charlie's basic incompetence as an attorney. In this case, any lawyer who'd passed the bar would have objected based on speculation. But Charlie didn't, because if there's one thing Charlie liked to do, it was talk about bullshit things that never happened.

He thought it over.

"You know, it's hard to say." Charlie threaded his fingers through his beard. "It's hard to say. Back then, it was all about the hippies, wasn't it, and that's a whole other kind of love. Their angels were the Doors and the Beatles. They had a lot of heavy music, man, those kids. They were all serious and angry, and you see what that got them. They still got thrown away and blown away, just like the good kids always are. And I'd have picked them up, you're right about that."

He shook his head regretfully.

"No Bee Gees, though? No strobes? No hustle? It mighta still happened, but I'll tell you this, Mr. Cozzi: it wouldn't have been as fun."

From *Night Fever: The Story of Charles Manson's Assault on the World*, by Vincenzo Cozzi (with Curt Gentry). W.W. Norton, 1980.

⌘

MANSON GUILTY
Manson, Kovacs, Englert Sentenced to Life without Parole
Wensinger Eligible After Forty Years

From the *New York Post*, July 3, 1979.

⌘

I was a wild child in the 60s like so many others. I smoked grass, dropped acid, woke up in places I didn't remember. I had ideas about what it meant to be free, and most of those ideas came from the music and men I thought I loved. If I was Violet's age in 1977, there's no telling what I'd have done for Charles Manson.

What I got that Violet Wensinger never did was the chance to fall in love with other things, including myself.

Some still call Violet "the Good One" of the Manson Family, but there's no question that she's where she belongs for killing Chip Auldridge, at least for now. Others say she's what happens when you're selfish enough to try to find yourself and someone else finds you first.

Disco was selfish and it was glamorous; it was silly and it was vain. It wasn't much worse than all the other dumb things we do to belong, all the terrible music we listen to. It was human, beautifully human, and on the edges of all human things there are the monsters who don't understand them.

Charles Manson couldn't dance, couldn't sing, couldn't play an instrument, could barely play records. In the end, he couldn't even kill. He found better people to do those things, and he did his best to find their worst.

Manson was an angry little man whose aching singularity of need for fame and appreciation could never be filled. It couldn't have been filled in the 1720s or the 1840s or the 1960s.

He was as inevitable to the 70s as an anvil falling from the sky, which is to say not at all.

> From "White Supremacists Can't Dance: The Mediocre Music of Manson," by Leslie Van Houten. *Rolling Stone*, December 1997.

155

⌘

Q: Ms. Wensinger, were you offered a plea agreement for your testimony here today?

A: Yes.

Q: Did you accept it?

A: No.

Q: Why?

A: Because I stabbed a man. Because I helped kill five others. Because now that I know everything Charlie is, everything he was wrong about, all the lies he told, even now I can look over at him at that table and see the spinning lights. I can hear the beginning of "Dancing Queen," and I'm afraid if he held out his hand to me, even now, I couldn't save myself from the beat.

From *Night Fever: The Story of Charles Manson's Assault on the World,* by Vincenzo Cozzi (with Curt Gentry). W.W. Norton, 1980.

S2E2: "Dark Horse Candidate"

Air Date: September 14, 1962
Writer: Hugh Kline
Director: Dean "Deano" McDonald

Synopsis: The unnamed President of the United States (James Agar) is on a goodwill tour of our allies in Eastern Europe when bad weather compels his flight to land in an obscure country unfortunately named "Krzalya." The storm forces the President's Secret Service agents to secure a nearby crumbling abbey to quarter him and his staff for the night, and the Special Agent in Charge Andrew Carlton (Richard Wyatt) finds no one living in the building though it has been wired for electricity.

It's a late night for the President as he consults with his re-election campaign manager (an uncharacteristically oily Leslie Nielsen) over brandy in a Medieval library. They discuss the dirty tricks they plan to use in the campaign against their "weak-livered" opponent, and they laugh the evening away and toast their ingenuity.

Carlton and the other agents patrol the grounds but their communications are limited by the thick stone walls. Several times, Wyatt believes he hears footsteps behind him and whirls with his gun drawn to find only a shadowed hallway, and clearly the atmosphere is getting to him. It doesn't help that he discovers dungeons and torture chambers clearly used within living memory.

157

In the small hours, a procession of cloaked figures winds through the corridor toward the President's room, and the agent on duty vainly fires his sidearm until he drops to the floor dead with his face twisted in a rictus scream. Other agents including Carlton approach but one of the figures stops them at the door with an admonishing hand.

Outside the room while the President shrieks on the other side, the specter tells Agent Carlton about the former master of the abbey, a cruel baron deposed in a "night of daggers" after decades of tyranny. Carlton listens only briefly before rushing inside the President's chamber.

There, the President is sitting up and calmly buttoning a shirt as he gets dressed. There are no screams and no evidence of the apparitions. Carlton asks if the President needs anything, and the President replies, "Yes, to get back home and back to making a difference."

In the final shot from the chamber, we hear the airplane taking to the now clear skies while the camera zooms in on the real President howling for help and shaking his dungeon chains.

Commentary: There was no shortage of political corruption even in 1962, but the pure anger of this episode presages that of the later Sixties. Several luminaries of the free speech and civil rights movements cited this episode as "a real mind-blower" from their childhoods and an inspiration for their lives of activism.

When asked years later about his inspiration for the episode, Hugh Kline sheepishly admitted that there was a mansion set available on a nearby soundstage from a Roger Corman film and one of an aircraft from a war picture, and he merely combined the two.

Poe at Gettysburg

When Edgar Usher Poe received word in the White House of the nearly 50,000 Union and Confederate casualties at Gettysburg, he is reported to have clutched his white tonsure of hair and collapsed to the floor crying, "Am I but the President of the Dead?"

I would not in my ignorance have guessed that when I wrote so often in my newspaper about his total unsuitability to the office. To me at my safe desk in Cincinnati, he was a Boston-born and Kentucky-raised man waging a slow and indecisive war with mixed loyalties. Until we made our brief acquaintance on that train journey to the Soldiers' National Cemetery, I had no conception that it was these fractures (and more besides) which made him whole.

Thirty years after his death, it is easy to forget in this celebration of his life that he had his weaknesses: prone to melancholy and hysteria, acidic in his words, quick to be slighted and slow to forgive it. He took the secession of the Southern states as a personal repudiation of his presidency, and he exulted in early Union victories—though not for long.

Yet we remember him today not for his clumsy military thinking or vindictive politics but for, of all things, a heart open and exposed to hurt. The man I met in that private car felt the death of strangers more acutely than any I've ever known. He lived in horror, not as its countryman but as a spy behind enemy lines.

I was there when he wrote his right and terrible Gettysburg Address, but no one believes me that I was no help at all—just present to watch him catch it, a cry and a paean and a curse all at once.

⌘

Seven and eighty years ago, our great progenitors conjured a nation with words, a tribe united not by coincidence of geography or inherited belief but upon ideals freely chosen. We are the nation that chose together to be a nation.

⌘

On November 18th, the President's chartered train left Washington for Gettysburg to dedicate the new cemetery there. I was among a dozen journalists aboard, watching the others play poker and drink brandy while I wrote a column for my newspaper. I don't remember much about that column except that it was almost certainly wrong.

What I do remember is that at 5:20 p.m., Poe's personal secretary John Newell entered the lounge, glanced over the heads of everyone there and caught me in his gaze. I froze and hunched slightly, wondering if the President's men had only just then realized who I was.

I began to gather my papers as he approached, wondering insanely if they'd slow the train down enough for me to step off or if I'd have to leap. Newell sidled past the other men who'd gone silent at his approach, and he leaned close to me.

"The President has requested to meet with you, sir," he said.

"With me?" I said, stupidly.

"Yes," he said.

"With George Youngston of the *Cincinnati Advertiser?*"

"Yes, sir," he said, guiding me to my feet with a gentle touch to the elbow. I gathered my bag with the papers sprayed from the top and followed him.

"Oh, Youngsy," said Fred Villiers from the Globe. "I hear they left one grave open just for you."

The other reporters laughed and I glanced back at them one more time before Newell guided me to the door. Newell knocked twice and, at the assent of a voice on the other side, swung it open for me.

What I saw first was what seemed to be a faceless man seated at a simple pine desk, and it took a moment for me to realize that the President of the fractured United States was holding his bald head in his hands above the scattered pages before him.

"You are the man on this train who hates me most, but you're the only one with a shred of fancy," said Poe.

⌘

In the decades since, we have brought men and women and children among us who had not the luxury of that choice, and we are now in the third year of a war deciding whether they are human. Ten thousand voices pro and con are now smothered by the blood-soaked soil beneath our feet, their words unintelligible from their shattered and fleshless jaws, their eyes blinded by eternal darkness, their hearts too still and silent. What they now know cannot help us, not even were we wise enough to listen.

163

⌘

I noticed a sharp pain in my knuckles from clutching my bag, and I willed myself to ease my grip.

"Sir," I said. "Mr. President. Your Excellency." My mind was flipping through every possible form of address, hoping one would be correct.

Poe looked up and squinted beneath his enormous pale brow. "Those are a far sight better than your usual names for me. 'Ol' Half-Heart.' 'The Turtle of War,' which I presume to be a reference to my features. 'Death's Usher.'"

"Sir, I—"

Newell stepped forward. "Can I get you anything, Mr. President?"

"No, thank you," Poe said. He coughed then in a burst so loud and concentrated that it made me step back.

"May I remind you that you haven't eaten since we left?"

I'd never seen Poe in person, but he indeed looked haggard and pale, his lips in their deep red the only color on his face. His deep-set eyes peered out from above dark and greasy smears. He seemed a skull atop a skeleton, and I was righter than I knew.

"I'm fine, Newell. You may go."

Newell did so, and I stood alone as far from the President's desk as I could.

"Mr. President," I said, "about those columns—"

"Are you about to tell me that I am not a 'a fourth-rate understudy who has not learned his lines' nor 'a Southern parasite gnawing at the blighted tree of liberty'?"

164

I didn't let myself wince, though I was surprised that Poe not only read but remembered my work. "I confess I say things sometimes more...largely...than I should."

"Largely," Poe said.

"I mean no disrespect, of course. One has to speak loudly sometimes to get the attention of others in a crowded room," I said.

"The room of people who despise me is crowded indeed, all of the South and half of the North."

"I don't...I don't despise you, sir," I said.

"It doesn't matter to me if you do," the President replied. "I want your help to write a speech that speaks...largely, as you might say."

"How largely?"

"Largely enough to end a war," the President said.

⌘

It is for us to decide why they died, and it is possible—even likely—that we may choose that they died for nothing. They certainly fought for nothing, trying to convince fools by the force of arms of what we already know and deny only for the sake of petulance: it is not the skin that makes a man better but his heart, and all of those are crimson.

To the eye of sufficient distance—distant Aidenn perhaps or a ship at sail between the stars—we are an amorphous mass of writhing gray worms feasting on a corpse, this mighty struggle as indistinguishable to that intelligence as the quarrels of ants are to us.

165

Our wars are not grand and heroic—they are small, and they are fought first between the heart that steers us true and the mind that we fill with the worst ideas of our loudest neighbors.

Most of us are losing.

⌘

At the President's gesture, I took a seat in a narrow wooden chair. Then he reached into the pocket of his waistcoat and withdrew a folded square of newsprint. It opened gently in his fingers like a butterfly.

"You assert here in your column from the sixteenth of February this year that—in your grandiloquent words—'a just Universe would never have elevated Poe to the presidency of these United States.'"

For a moment I marveled that a man of such stature would carry my words on his person, enjoyed even a moment of pride, but then my face surged with heat.

"Mr. President, I find it vindictive in the extreme that you would summon a man from the press to admonish him for exercising his right to free expression."

"Mr. Youngston," he said. "You are not here to be admonished. You are here because I agree with you."

"Sir?"

"I have felt for some time like a man stretched taut across his years like the skin of a drum, sensitive to subtle vibrations, ready to tear at the slightest excess of pressure," Poe said. "What I want to know, Mr. Youngston, is how you perceived it."

I have written perhaps a million words in the decades since my meeting with President Poe, and it still took me more than half of them to learn that there is a kind of drunkenness one gets from the beauty of words on a page, an addiction to their sounds, and that there is nothing so sobering as having to repeat them to the face of a living human being. That lesson began on my way to Gettysburg.

"It was hyperbole, sir, nothing more. It sounded true but wasn't."

"What is truth but the beautiful sound of it? You listened closely and I want to know what you heard."

"As I reflect on it now, I'm not sure any man is suited to the office of President in a war."

He waved that off. "But I am singularly unsuited. Why?"

What was it I had perceived, truly? Nothing. I'd seen between what others saw and reported, that was all. A man who thought overlong. A man more wounded by words than by death. A man morbidly paralyzed by his office.

"It is my impression, Mr. President, that you seem a man of deeper feeling than action."

Poe smiled at that, actually smiled in a way unsettling to the extreme, and he clapped his hands together with a dull, weak clopping noise. "There it is, Mr. Youngston. There it is! I am a watcher of men, not their leader—sail more than engine?"

"That is an eloquent way to state it."

"I find myself in this place not from my own propulsion but by a long series of accidents and coincidences, Mr. Youngston. You know of the circumstances of my birth?"

"Yes, sir. Born to celebrated actors in Boston who died tragically early and raised by friends of the family, theater owners from whom you take your middle name."

"Quite true, though it was my mother who was justly celebrated and my father justly uncelebrated. She died of consumption, as did my beloved Virginia. We are a family cursed to die of civil wars in the blood."

I had already guessed the signs of his malady, but that confirmed them.

"Hardly a Presidential origin, wouldn't you agree? Had they lived, I might have been a third-rate actor on a stage instead of a fourth-rate one in the White House. Would my signature role be Hamlet or Macbeth?"

I desperately hoped the question was rhetorical but as the silence limped on, I realized it wasn't. "Neither, I'd hope?" I tried.

"Both, more likely," Poe said. "As I am now, the feckless cowardly prince and the conniving madman."

"I wouldn't say—"

"I consider every day that my life comes down to the choice of a single hour above my mother's corpse in a Richmond theater dressing room. Had the Ushers been harder to find, had they said no...I could be a Virginian, dead or wearing gray. Had they been lawyers instead of theater owners, I might have been a rebellious actor instead of a rebellious lawyer."

The difference in the President had been slight enough; his early fame had come from dramatic closing soliloquies, including one that would have saved Oliver Dew from the gallows if he'd been white. What made Poe popular (beside his youthful orations) were the many stories of his passionate, nearly deranged fights for lost causes. I'd had written once that the Union was too important to be another of them, but with the man now sitting in front of me, I started to wonder.

"I suspect all thinking beings consider their lives that could have been, but I..." He formed a frame with his fingers in the air. "I can see mine as through a soot-streaked window. I feel most acutely a second Poe who walks a half step ahead or behind me always, just out of my reach. I wonder often if he is the better Poe, the one not losing scores of his countrymen."

"Is it not as likely, sir, that you are the better Poe? Your career, your accomplishments..."

The President seemed as surprised as I was to hear me say that. He tapped his finger to his temple.

"I see his dreams, Youngston. He goes farther at night than I do, and more importantly, farther also by day."

⌘

I am a man born in the North and raised in the South. I have kissed white-gloved hands in ballrooms and waded barefoot in creeks with the children of slaves. I've had the fortune of two homes and the misfortune that their people now hate each other, with some of their dead rotting over there and others rotting over here, sharing the same oblivion.

By now, their blood has seeped and trickled its way to the hideous heart at the center of the Earth, the one that feeds on our death and suffering because those are the most common nutrients we produce. It thrums stronger in all our violent stupidity, and when reason dares to whisper, it sings hatred to us in our dreams.

The flavor of our deaths, the flags that waved above them, make us no less a delicacy – only a varied one.

⌘

The President coughed again. "I am not as well as I appear," he said, a shocking statement given how poorly he did.

"I regret very much to hear that, sir," I said. "Are your physicians hopeful?"

"Do you think they should be?"

I thought briefly of a platitude, some assurance that with faith and tenacity, there could be hope. Yet there was nothing

169

more absurd to say to the man before me with skin so wan that it was nearly translucent.

"Perhaps not," I said finally.

"It is not a cause for melancholy, I assure you. The war is drawn to me as surely as iron filings to a magnet. I must take it with me when I go, and you must help me."

"I will do all that I am able, sir." From my satchel I removed a sheet of paper, a pen, and my inkwell.

The President smiled. "Is it that easy for you to free the words from your brain? Me, I need a hatchet and even then reach but one half the dreams afloat in my imagination."

"Perhaps it is an issue of practice," I said.

⌘

Our nation is a mansion of many-colored rooms built upon that blood-soaked sand, and the cracks to our foundation have widened now past deniability. We have danced in those rooms oblivious to the loping specter of our national pestilence outside, and now it walks among us. It is an apparition masked with poisonous blood, and as our national host, it falls to me to expose and confront it.

We must accept the ravages of our illness, and I must be first. We can but hope our blood is not exhausted before we win.

⌘

170

By that moment in our conversation, the sweat on the President's brow was flowing down his forehead and toward his exhausted eyes. He closed them and blotted himself with a red-flecked handkerchief, and when he lowered his hand, he did not open them.

I waited as long as I could, though only a matter of seconds, before saying, "Mr. President?" rather stridently.

"I'm still here, Youngston, though 'here' is not what it once was."

Knowing time was running short not only for our journey but for his, I leaned forward. "Tell me what you see, Mr. President."

He swallowed, eyes still closed. Then, slowly, he said, "I see a great mansion sliding into a tarn."

I wrote down his dreams.

⌘

That sullen phantasm before us has come to collect the debt of ideals we borrowed with usurious interest. We shall pay now or we shall pay forever more, the maddened nation that fell shrieking into the abyss of history, a warning to all others of what comes when heart and action disagree.

The truth I now acutely perceive is this: we are a nation of liars. We say and write many things—all men are created equal, for example—that we hope become true simply from our inspired utterance. We practice an American voodoo, a desperate faith that by changing the signs, we change the universe.

Every one of these men died because we are liars, and our only possible virtue is that we labor harder to make our lies become true.

171

⌘

When we arrived in Gettysburg, Newell and Secretary Seward were so aghast at the President's haggard and feverish appearance that they pleaded for him to return to Washington and wait to dedicate the next cemetery instead of this one.

It was that suggestion of another time and another cemetery that invigorated Poe enough to take quarters in town and even nod solemnly at the bullet holes we were shown in the walls on the way. I prepared to take my leave, but he bade me to stay and so I did in the parlor of the house with his secretary in a long vigil.

The next morning, he was strong enough after a late breakfast to walk most of the way to the dedication ceremony without our assistance. He paused once to hover his hand near to the ground, and we rushed forward to prevent a fall that didn't come. He rose slowly from his haunches, and we guided him the rest of the way to the platform and up the steps and to a waiting chair. There he sat sweat-dreaming while the Honorable Edward Everett prattled on for two agonizing hours with his own oration.

⌘

Though we earned this horror, there is yet a feeble gleam of hope. All diseases must end, either in death or in health. We cannot predict or contain the raging of most afflictions, but we can contain this one. We can decide that these men moldering around us are enough. We can honor their sacrifice by making them nearly the last. We can lie to ourselves that the debt of blood is paid, and then we can work for the rest of our nation's life to make it true.

We can choose that there will be only one more casualty of our national disease.

⌘

When the Baltimore Glee Club finished their "Consecration Chant," Poe did not immediately rise. He took two deep inhalations and clutched the arms of his chair, and only when Secretary Seward held it in place could he stand. He then thumped his way across the wooden planks with laborious steps.

It was my great privilege to watch the President of the United States deliver the Gettysburg Address at his personal invitation, and when I am asked to tell what happened that day, I little recall the tone of his voice or the motions of his arms. What I remember instead are the faces of his audience, the people who started by fanning themselves with hats and ended as frozen in place as the dead, their jaws agape, their eyes wide.

Scholars debate how much of that address was written by the President and how much was written by me, and none of them believe that it was neither of us—that the speech came from somewhere or someone else and used him as its mouth and lungs. I know nothing of that other man, the one the President summoned on that dais, except that he lived in such darkness that our lives were the light.

I was the man who caught the President when he died, and I was the one who heard his final whispered word among the screams of the crowd. I have never revealed that word and I never will, though like our nation, it too is a compound of two ideas, the first a negative and the last a hope. It was the perfect word to end a war, and it did though only I heard it.

He wanted the speech to be what we remember instead, and so it shall be.

173

⌘

True, I have been nervous and I have been mad, and I have swirled in maelstroms and trembled in awe at the grotesque and dreary fancies that visit me in the night. I am perhaps the worst of all possible presidents and almost certainly the worst of all possible Poes, but it is and has been my great honor to walk beside you all in our kingdom by the sea. My heart has grown swollen and loud—can you not hear its hideous rhythm?—with the blood of better men, and I take it now with me to be held dear wherever next I go.

As for myself, I am simply Edgar Usher Poe, the President of the United States—and this is my last duty.

S2E8: "Neither Seen Nor Heard"

Air Date: October 25, 1962
Writer: David Findley
Director: Chester Gee

Synopsis: Nine-year-old Paulie (played by Edwin
Martinsbrook, later of *Circus Train!* fame) grudgingly drags a
battered trash can to the curb of his house, and it's his bad
luck that it tumbles over with the garbage rolling everywhere.
He stuffs it back in muttering to himself until he comes upon
a woman's wig. In black-and-white, it's hard to tell but the wig
is clearly damp with a dark fluid, probably blood.

Paulie turns it over in his hands, considers, and then places it
atop his head. He is then stricken with a terrible vision of a
silhouetted figure strangling a someone in a hotel room. He
drops to his knees in the gutter and claws first at his neck
with no effect but then at the wig instead. As soon as it comes
off, he can breathe again.

He gets his bike and rides off with the wig while his father
watches from the window. Paulie takes it to the police station
and asks Officer Boggs about it, but he shrugs and says
nobody's reported a woman missing a wig. He goes next to his
minister, Father Rudy, who encourages him to pray for
guidance on the right thing to do. He takes it that evening to
a Boy Scout meeting, and the boys throw it around over his
head.

175

On his way home from the Scout meeting, he pedals into the parking lot of a low-rate hotel. He stops almost in a trance at room 151 and tries the door. It swings open and he steps into the dark room.

What ensues next has been subject to decades of debate. That week's "Steube on the Tube" column in the *LA Times* called it a "surreal animated frenzy not unlike a Man Ray nightmare," stop-motion triangles swirl around one another under strobe lights until a slam cut returns us to live action. Paulie, wearing the wig with his hands soaked in blood, staggers from the motel room in shock. Absently, he places the wig into another trash can and cycles home.

Commentary: The rumor of the origin for this episode is that David Findley found an actual wig in a Los Angeles gutter and wore it to the Derby. He claimed later that the stories he wrote while wearing it were "orgiastic bacchanals of decadence and grotesquery," to which Barry Weyrich replied, "Who could tell?"

The animated sequence from this episode turned out to be deeply influential on avant garde art of the Seventies, and David Lynch is reported to have used a personally colorized version as the backdrop for an early kinetic sculpture called "Man's Mind on Wedding Bells."

Story Notes

Acres of Perhaps

Even though this is my second book themed around a television show, I promise I didn't watch that much as a kid.

I grew up in a time when TV shows played on their own schedules, and if you missed them—because you were in school or they were canceled or your dad was watching *Benny Hill*—they were more or less gone. A lot of the shows I "remember" from my childhood are very different in my memory than reality, either because I read their novelizations first (James Blish's *Star Trek* adaptations are ten times better than the show), or because I wrote whole seasons of them in my head. My *Alfred Hitchcock Presents* is a lot different than yours.

What I did watch every day after school on WTBS was even weirder: *Leave it to Beaver*. I was fascinated by such a strange family where Ward would repair the toaster's electric plug with a little good-natured scolding for June about pulling it out by the cord instead of, say, beating her with it like would happen in our house. Ward never hauled off and punched the Beav, and June never lost a pair of glasses to a smack in the face.

Even for the time, though, the Cleavers were a weird fucking family. For one thing, they were called "the Cleavers" like some butcher ancestor from Alsace got renamed coming through Ellis Island. For another, Beav had a strange habit (like

177

me) of imbuing non-sentient things with sentience, like that time he stole a tree from his old house because he was worried it was lonely for being left behind.

"You really think trees have feelings, Beaver?" his friend Larry asks.

"All the trees in Mr. Disney's pictures have feelings. They yell and scream and chase people around and everything."

"Aw, that's just in cartoons. Did you ever have a real tree screaming at you?"

"No."

But he thinks about it first, and in that pause is everything I write about.

Probably the biggest influence on my writing from television, beyond the thirty total episodes of *The Twilight Zone* and *Alfred Hitchcock Presents* and *The Outer Limits* I saw as a kid, comes from this idea that the world is plenty strange without the supernatural if you're perceptive enough. When Beaver Cleaver grew up, he must have found a home in a little Washington town called Twin Peaks. With a name like "Beaver," how could he not?

My fiction tends to appear in genre magazines, and I'm proud of that. I get a lot of feedback, though, from readers that I don't "go far enough" or include enough of a "speculative element," that my stories tend to be more about people imagining the supernatural or strange than experiencing it. Maybe my imagination is too shriveled or stunted to jump all in on a good monster or secondary world, or maybe I've gotten a little too good at making this world more entertaining to me with delusion.

Whatever the cause, I'm more fascinated (or perhaps *desperate* is the word) to see signs of the wondrous in the ordinary that still satisfy my regrettably cynical nature. I want to believe, as Agent Fox Mulder would say.

As I wrote this story, I wondered about the schism in myself between workaday magic (the Barry Weyrich kind) and "inspiration," which David Findley relies upon. I've spent too much of my life pursuing the fast and sexy variety while overlooking the kind that lives in jobs and marriages and mowing the lawn. But as I look through my work, I'm hard-pressed to even remember which stories came about in a sudden burst of lightning and which only trickled in, and I certainly can't tell the difference between them in quality.

My conclusion? I think they're largely the same magic, and one just moves more slowly than the other.

Originally appeared in *Asimov's Science Fiction*, July 2015, and *The Year's Best Fantasy and Science Fiction: 2016 Edition*, Rich Horton, ed.

The Zodiac Walks on the Moon

I first read Robert Graysmith's book *Zodiac* when I was fourteen years old, and there's no question that the titular serial killer figured prominently in the origins of my imagination. For one thing, he seemed to be a crazed criminal genius, sending taunting letters and arcane cryptograms to the newspapers that showed a strange erudition with topics ranging from Gilbert and Sullivan to celestial navigation.

179

For another, his composite drawing looked very much like my father at the time of the crimes, a big square head with a crewcut and horn-rimmed glasses. Though I consciously knew that my father couldn't possibly be the Zodiac, the notion helped me adjust to the horrible truth that it was possible for a man as smart as my father to use that intelligence for evil, and that however violent and embarrassing his crimes were, I could at least take consolation that he was, after all, a criminal genius.

I guess that's all you need to know about my childhood, that I wished my father was the Zodiac because he was the BETTER choice.

As time went on, however, I realized that when you examined the Zodiac case carefully, it was just as likely that he was a lucky idiot as a mastermind. So much of the more sophisticated elements of Zodiac's crimes, the use of radians and astrology and movie lore and military tactics, could be Graysmith's interpretations of ambiguous stimuli. If anything, Zodiac's crimes were the lowest-hanging fruit he could find, culminating in shooting a cab driver in the back of the head like a common mugger. He delivered on none of his threats and eventually faded into obscurity.

By an interesting coincidence, the "lucky idiot" theory made more sense to me after re-contacting my father after twenty years of silence. He too seemed like someone who'd mastered the sound of being smart without any of the substance, and that was an important lesson for me.

Sometimes we can't figure a person out not because we can't raise ourselves to his genius but because we can't lower ourselves to his mediocrity.

The story in this collection largely came about because I reflected on the interesting coincidence that the Zodiac stepped up his public game after the Moon landings, and I wondered what inspiration someone like that would take from our greatest human achievement.

Like Graysmith, I think I've given Zodiac way more credit than he likely deserves.

Originally appeared in *Nightmare Magazine*,
November 2017.

The Leaning Lincoln

This story is slightly true.

In 1983, my father almost certainly wound up an emotionally-troubled man into a shooting spree to kill their mutual enemies — creditors, bankers, and a lawyer.

The man started by fatally shooting his own lawyer (whom he saw as "mishandling" an inheritance case) and was luckily stopped there, but when he was arrested, he was found with a list of other victims not obviously connected to him. He never admitted they were connected to my father.

[I won't comment on the specifics of the real case out of respect for the victim and his family. I hope I fictionalized it enough not to be offensive, and I hope that though I humanized the killer, I didn't absolve him of his crime. He was definitely responsible for his own deranged reasons, but there's a truth most people didn't know which is that my father helped derange him.]

The man — fictionalized as "Henry" in the story — was kinder and more understanding to me and my family than my father ever was. He took us to the movies and talked about

Dungeons and Dragons with me, and yes, he did make me a lead Abraham Lincoln figurine that seemed to bring me bad luck.

As a kid playing with action figures on the back patio, I heard my dad rant to "Henry" about his enemies while "Henry" quietly listened, and in the decades since, I've wondered what I should have done or whom I could have told. "Henry" was convicted and died in prison while my father went on to other crimes. He's dead now, too.

The speculation in this story is the idea that a kid like me, weird and dreamy and superstitious, could find a way to use that to do good in the real world.

I wanted to talk about where magic came from with other readers like me who I know wonder that for themselves. I wanted to talk about how our books and comics and movies and action figures saved a lot of us from terrible things, and I wanted to talk about what we should do with that to pass it on, how we should add science fiction and fantasy to the world instead of just hiding there.

That's what Scott does in the story, and it's what I couldn't quite manage when I was ten. I had to go back in time for another shot at putting my father on trial and convicting him with magic.

182

Originally appeared in *Asimov's Science Fiction*, October-November 2016.

Night Fever

A question that's hard to answer for me is where I'm from. I spent the first five years of my childhood in Garden City, New

York, the second five in Englewood, Florida, and the third five in Arcadia, Florida. That makes me a curious combination of a 1970s New Yorker, an early 1980s beach-side Floridian, and a late 1980s anti-redneck punk.

Because the point of the question is to get a better sense of who I am as a person, I usually just say I'm from New York even though I left fairly early because my family kind of carried New York with us even to Florida. My mother kept her accent and my father kept his attitude, and I always suspected I was missing out by living in the sticks of Florida.

What I remember from my childhood about New York is that it was fast and it was gray and it was dirty; my mother once admonished me for kissing a train to thank it for carrying us safely to our destination. I remember my sister listening to Shaun Cassidy and Barry Manilow on the radio, I remember playgrounds with black rubber mats atop the concrete, I remember the lights of Rockefeller Center at Christmas, and I remember my grandparents' house in Flushing. I remember visiting my father at his job at OTB (which I thought was a bank because of how he dressed), and I remember going to Pathmark next door.

I knew one day I'd write about my New York, though I had no idea when or how.

Then one day I posted an off-hand tweet that if Charles Manson had been active in the 1970s instead of the 1960s, it would have been Night Fever coming down fast instead of Helter Skelter. My friend and Clarion classmate Robert Levy said he'd read a story about that, and I immediately deleted the tweet to save the idea for myself.

I was scared to write the story because I wanted it to be authentic. I knew a lot about the Manson case and it was fun to extrapolate it into the 1970s, but I was nervous that my exposure to the city wasn't enough. My sister spent her time at violin lessons, not Studio 54.

When I started my research, I was surprised at how quickly the things I discovered clicked with my memories of big heavy cars and trash-blown streets, and somehow it wasn't that hard to feel back at home there. The story didn't exactly write itself, but it was a comfortable place for most of the work.

If there's a point to the story, it's that blaming the Sixties for the Manson crimes is absurd—a person like that would use the tools of any era to assert his will, and there are always forgotten and isolated people to recruit. Leslie Van Houten has a cameo in the story as a journalist because that's where I suspect she might have ended up if she hadn't met Manson.

Do I think she should be released? I am certain she (and her other female codefendants) would do no harm if they were out. As for whether that serves the cause of "justice," I'm not sure we know enough of their hearts either way.

Originally appeared in *Asimov's Science Fiction*,
May-June 2017.

Poe at Gettysburg

I was lucky during my senior year at the University of Florida to take a course with Poe scholar William Goldhurst, a large man with much gusto who used to pronounce the author's name "POW!" It was an evening class, and after his great lectures and readings, it was fun to walk in the dark across campus and live inside my mental Poeland, though it's hard to properly brood in shorts and a Gator t-shirt.

Something that surprised me as an English major was how boring the classes were. I enjoyed writing and I enjoyed reading, but the only classes available in that large and busy department during my registration appointments were hard to stitch together with my interests, stuff like 17th century drama and 18th century diarists. It was the class in Poe and another in science fiction that saved my interest in studying literature, and I'm not sure if that's a blessing or not.

For Goldhurst's class as an undergrad and in later graduate ones, I researched Poe a great deal—I might well have made him my specialty if I continued in academia—and I always found it fascinating that he took the name "Usher" for his celebrated story from a family that were friends of his parents.

They were theater owners, and I wondered what would have happened if they'd adopted him instead of the Allans. The Poe we discover in his letters was embarrassingly whiny and petulant, and it's hard to tell what part of that was inborn and what came from his early (and late) abandonments. Would his life have been better or worse with the Ushers? For him or for us?

Poe, like Lincoln, was born in 1809 which means that he could plausibly have survived to see the horrors of the Civil War. Some Poe scholars call his view of slavery "complicated," but it was no more complicated than that of many others raised in Virginia: he didn't think that much about it if he didn't have to, and when he did, he didn't view it as unnatural. He took on the opinions of the people around him (at least in that) because they were convenient.

If he'd been raised in Kentucky with the real Usher family, there's no guarantee that his thinking would have been any

185

more liberal. Lincoln was born there, and he came somewhat slowly to his abolitionist views.

There are two reasons I gave Poe the chance to be a hero in this story. The first is that I wanted to play with the idea that we believe what we believe often because of the coincidence of where we're born, not from logic or reason.

The second, and more important, is that it was far more fun to write his speech as President of the United States instead of President of the Confederacy because fuck those guys.

Original to this collection.

Acknowledgements

Thanks first to you for reading this book all the way to here and still wanting more. That's some persistence, and I admire it.

This book wouldn't exist at all without the nudging of Steve Berman, CEO of Lethe Press, who reminds me that I actually do have a career even when I'd rather not think about it.

I'd also like to thank David Lally for providing the cover image for this book, perfectly capturing the feel I was going for. What most people don't know is that he didn't need to dress up at all to look like that. I'd also like to thank his wife Tina's gams, also pictured on the cover.

Some of the earliest readers and listeners to these stories encouraged me to go on, and I'm grateful especially to Robert Stutts and Angela Still on that score. All the usual suspects (Tom Phillips, Don Rochester, Ray Rodil, Arnold Cassell, Kelley Vanda, Scott McClellan, Richard Soehner, Lillian Soehner, Mac McDonald, and William Simmons) heard several of these as a test audience, so they share the blame.

For perhaps the first time in my life, I work at a day job that actually contributes to my creativity and mental well-being instead of sapping it, and I'm grateful for the encouragement of Pete Martinez, Pamela Boggs, Todd Slifka, Derree Braswell, Amy Schneider, and the rest of the team.

187

I'm grateful that Sheila Williams at *Asimov's Science Fiction* and John Joseph Adams at *Nightmare Magazine* saw the potential in some of these stories to publish them originally and offer editorial suggestions that made them way better.

My family, as always, has provided the rich water table of the bizarre which I continue to plumb, everyone from my sister Karen Simpson and her husband Marty to my nieces Katie and Emily and my brother Andrew.

I've already dedicated the book to my mother, but I wanted to say again how much I've appreciated my mother's absolute, all-in belief that I should be doing this shit with my life. The cancer may have taken her body, but she's left enough of her spirit in me to last many more years and many more stories.

And of course, Aimee Payne is the person with whom I've made just the life I need to make stories like these. She's the reason I don't have to choose between imagination and the real world anymore.

About the Author

Will Ludwigsen's fiction of "weird mystery" has appeared in places like *The Year's Best Science Fiction and Fantasy*, *Alfred Hitchcock's Mystery Magazine*, *Asimov's Science Fiction*, *Strange Horizons*, *Weird Tales*, *Nightmare*, *Lightspeed*, and many others.

He lives in Jacksonville, Florida, with his partner, writer Aimee Payne.